Night's Harbor

Night's Harbor

W.J. Renehan

A Division of New Street Communications, LLC

Wickford, RI

Published 2015

Dark Hall Press
A Division of New Street Communications, LLC
Wickford, RI

Cover Art:
"Vampire" by Edvard Munch

For Bram Stoker:
This return to roots.

The house itself was unremarkable, seated on the outskirts of an abandoned village north of Brasov, nestled into the shadowed foothills of those ancient steeps, the Carpathians. Its gutters sagged, brimming with the leaves and branches of unkempt seasons, decayed so that new life had begun to take root in the old, green shoots rising from the filth. Its roof, little more than a carpet of mosses, had fallen through in places, surrendering to the weight of snows, the dance of rains. The yard, wildly overgrown, was more of a field, nettle blown and vine choked. Now late spring, the cicadas sang nightly revels to its majesty.

That the house of death should be covered in life was no small irony, and certainly not lost on those who moved there. Indeed, almost nothing was lost on them.

Jacobi stood on the ground floor, peering through a gap in the boarded front window. The moon was full, bathing the yard in silver light.

"Why did he not call us sooner, brother?" Mara asked from her seat in the darkness. "All those years, thinking him dead."

"You know better than to question him," Jacobi said without turning.

"I'm questioning you, brother."

"I don't presume to know his mind."

"But you wonder, just as I."

Jacobi turned from the window, the slanting moonlight illuminating the ghostly whiteness of his face.

"Yes."

Movement sounded from the second floor, and he removed his pocket watch to check the time.

Before his turning, Jacobi had been many things; a son, a brother, a soldier. He'd also been a rapist and murderer of women and children, though never caught. But first and perhaps foremost in his own mind, he had been a maker and repairer of clocks.

Back when time held meaning.

Still, he kept his old pocket watch with him, polishing its silver body, winding it each day with obsessive diligence.

As he checked it now—12:38—it occurred to him that time, at least for the moment, had reclaimed a small measure of its previous sway.

"It's my turn," he said.

He took the stairs to the second floor slowly, because he knew how much that frightened it.

Had he remembered to feed it the night before? He wasn't certain. He scooped a dish into a bag of dog food before pushing the door open into the dark. There came the sound of hurried movement at his entrance as the thing crawled into a corner, panting. This made his insides feel light and fluttery, and he could not help but smile as he sparked a lantern to burning life.

Oh, how it trembled at the sight of him, and he felt himself growing hard as his eyes roamed over its corrugated flesh.

What tales its scars told. He knew them intimately, as true obsession knows every radiant inch of its object.

Here was devotion. Here was nurturance.

The eyes he'd left, but the lids, the tongue, the hands and feet he'd taken. Its sex, though once female, was no longer distinguishable, no more than a lump of scarred-over tissue. He'd taken particular time with that.

"Is it hungry?" he asked.

It moaned unintelligibly, raising stumps to cover its face.

He slid the dish across the bare boards, and seeing that he meant no immediate harm, it began to chew up the kibble in great mouthfuls.

He walked to it slowly and stroked its head while it ate. There was still hair in scraggly patches where he'd not burned it. The blowtorch had always played second fiddle to the blade, but still, they'd had their moments.

"It shouldn't have interfered," he said quietly, the ruined creature nodding in submission. "It made a mistake there."

It whimpered, tears running down its face.

Jacobi sighed, removing a butterfly knife from his pocket, opening it with an effortless flick of the wrist.

This one had proved resourceful; had caused them more

than a little trouble. Not a trained slayer—an apprentice maybe—but a nuisance none the less. Still, perhaps he'd bled it for too long. Father deserved fresher sustenance.

"I don't suppose it was working with others? It would be shown mercy in exchange for their location."

It shook its head—out of what? Ignorance? Surely not defiance. No, they'd moved out of that country some time ago.

"Very well," he said, grabbing it by what was left of its hair and sliding a plastic bucket before it. "Dream of sweet things."

It did not struggle, long resigned to what was coming.

He opened its throat, the bucket catching most of the crimson rush, and then upended the body so as to empty it completely.

He would bury it out back with the others later.

The stairs to the basement creaked as Jacobi led, Mara following. The air was much cooler down there, as the Master preferred it.

Mara lit candles about the dank room as Jacobi set about removing the lid from the long crate and clearing the black earth from what lay beneath.

The shriveled, crusted lips parted just enough to receive the feeding tube, long white fingers clutching greedily about its end as Jacobi began to funnel the blood.

Hibernation had left Lement weak. His fangs had recessed for lack of nourishment; his black eyes stared from sunken, yellowed pits; long, pointed ears lay flat against the bald dome of his skull. His features were vulpine.

The feeding done, Jacobi and Mara knelt before the crate with reverence.

Licking blood from his lips, Lement settled back into the black earth.

"My... my children... have many questions," he rasped between ragged inhalations of breath. "Come... I did not choose either of you... for your timidity."

Mara stroked the old monster's brow.

"Why did you leave us, father?"

"Yes, father," Jacobi said. "Why?"

"I had to go to ground... for what's coming... Neither of you could know where... for reasons you already know."

"What is coming, father?" Mara asked, moving closer.

"Our dominion," he said, touching her face with a gnarled, translucent claw. She kissed it, lovingly.

He turned his ancient gaze to Jacobi then.

"And not unlike the Christian God," he hissed, a nictitating membrane flashing across his eyes, "my son goeth before me."

Night in Graves Harbor comes on with the same listless magic as in any other small New England town; an unremarkable sense of quieting, offering both the warmth of routine and the cold ache of banality.

This one was no different.

Monique Andrews drew on her cigarette as she shuttered the town's general store for the night, her thoughts tiredly shifting between her deadbeat husband—who was by that time passed out drunk on their couch—and her aching knees, which had been giving her increasing trouble of late. She stared out across Main and beyond into the harbor. The last boats were on their way in, the blinking channel markers bobbing on swells of black beneath a darkling sky.

Jackson Coombs threw her a wave from the garage of his auto-repair shop across the way, about ready to close up for the day himself.

Monique sighed, crushing out her spent butt and returning

the small gesture with a weary smile.

Down Main the Harborside Diner was full of its usual clatter and dash, young Sophia Reardon running herself ragged from table to table, the smell of chowder and clam cakes permeating the air.

Three streets over the Reverend Thomson swung from a tree bench in the First Methodist churchyard. Striking a match, he fired up a pipe of cherry tobacco, admiring the last glorious rays of sunset.

Coasting the rutted back roads skirting town, Grace Dreger and several school friends passed a joint and a bottle they'd hey-buddied from the Indian liquor store, doing their best to forget just who and where they were.

Out off the northern end of Purgatory Road, Tom Brockton's bar was beginning to fill up, the jukebox pumping out a familiar chain of rock and country standards. "Crimson and Clover" drifted ghostily through the surrounding woods, augmented by the drunken accompaniment of patrons.

Somewhere someone was struck.

Somewhere someone received good news.

Somewhere someone was learning to give up.

The town hummed with thoughts recurring, desires habituating, and the first stars were glinting the sky when Sam Peters began to arrange the flowers on his wife's grave, removing the decayed remnants of previous offerings, a dull tightness welling in his throat.

Evil, in all its scarlet subtleties, its arabesque designs, always thrives upon the presence of structure and routine. For the currency of evil is horror—and true, sheering, midnight horror at its most base lies not in chaos, but in order. Like the scheduling of cattle cars through barbed gates, how easily the structures and machinery we have built our worlds upon may turn against us—and what is worse still: how quietly they turn.

Night fell over Graves Harbor like a funeral shroud.

Earl Buxton took a swig of whiskey from his flask behind a stack of lobster traps as Cal Norris went about readying the boat for their run.

"Come on, Earl. Let's get moving."

Earl slid the flask into the inner pocket of his jean jacket, coming around to throw off the bowline. He walked back and threw off the stern, stepping aboard. The deck was wet and he lost his footing, slamming his tailbone on the railing.

"Dammit!"

"You all right?" Cal asked from the wheelhouse.

"Shit. Yeah, just let me sit for a minute."

Cal emerged from the cabin with a mug of coffee. "You might think about laying off the sauce on these runs," he said, regarding the man. "Can smell it on you from here."

Earl waved him off dismissively.

Cal pressed. "You know I'm no one to judge, but if it's going to affect your—"

"It won't," Earl cut him off. "Just give me a minute."

"I mean it," Cal said. "You're an old friend, and I'm happy to throw you some work, but I need you to keep your head on straight for this shit. If you're gonna come out here lit—"

"It won't be a problem."

"All right then. Let's get to it."

Cal slipped back into the wheelhouse as Earl stood, rubbing his backside.

Prick, Earl thought. *Who else you gonna convince to raid traps with you?*

He made his way into the cabin to join Cal. They were underway now, bow pointed between the channel buoys and out past the breakwater.

Cal handed him a cup of coffee.

"You should have some."

"Thanks," Earl said, accepting. He lit a cigarette and took a seat, alternating drags and sips of the cheap, lukewarm coffee.

"So what did you get up to last night?" Cal asked.

Earl mulled this over, thin tendrils of smoke curling from his nostrils.

"Spent most of the night at Brockton's. Was a good crowd. There were a couple of girls there from out of town. Forget her name, but this brunette ended up coming home with me."

"No shit?" Cal replied, though he doubted the truth of this. He couldn't imagine the sort of woman who'd entertain the thought of sleeping with Earl, never mind one who would actually go through with it.

"Yes sir," Earl confirmed, a sly grin on his face.

He *had* taken a brunette home, a decent looking one at that, but only for a half an hour, and it had set him back about a hundred and fifty dollars. He'd kept going soft through it and had a terrible time finishing. It had been more embarrassing than enjoyable, but these were not details he wished to share.

Old limp-dick Buxton. The most useless POS in Rhode Island.

"Yeah," Earl mumbled, almost to himself. "Bitch was wild."

He could still hear the girl's soft laughter as she left his one bedroom shit-can of a house.

They were approaching the breakwall, the moon reflecting on the rolling water. There wasn't much chop, which Earl was thankful for, still a tad woozy from the previous night. The coffee and cigarette were steadying him though.

The first set of traps went by quickly, and by the sixth Earl was feeling more like himself. Cal flipped on an oldies rock station and soon they were moving along at a steady clip.

"Probably make it in early tonight," Cal remarked, surveying their haul. "Beers on me, yeah?"

Earl smiled, setting an empty trap down on the railing, and threw the man a mock salute. As he turned to toss the trap over, he thought he glimpsed something in the dark.

"Hey Cal, you see that?"

Cal turned to where Earl was pointing just as the boat appeared, drifting from out the gloom.

It was an old fishing vessel, the swirling, sea-green letters spread across its rusted hull reading: *Emilija.*

No running light shone, nor was there any movement on

deck or in the wheelhouse.

"Jesus, Cal. She's a ghost."

"We'll see about that," Cal said, motoring alongside their discovery and cutting the engine. "Get a flashlight."

Earl retrieved one from the forward compartment, handing it off.

"Maybe we ought to just leave it be."

"Chicken shit," Cal laughed, climbing the wheelhouse and stepping off onto the boat. He shined the flashlight back in Earl's face. "You stay right there, sweetie. Poppa Cal will make sure it's safe."

He turned, and when he saw what was there to be seen, a chain of screams leapt from him, carrying over the black, churning swells.

Slatted morning light spilled through the partially drawn shades of the living room where Sam Peters sat, eyeing the two objects on the low table before him.

He picked up the pill bottle and stared idly at its label.

SAMUEL PETERS, PAXIL, 40 MILLIGRAMS.

TAKE 1 TABLET BY MOUTH ONCE DAILY.

He set the bottle back down, his hand moving to the second object.

He hadn't fired the Colt in years, but he liked to hold it sometimes. His fingers traced its cold steel contours, from grip to barrel, over the serial numbers like braille.

He lay back on the couch, his eyes shifting between the gun and the pill bottle.

Pain or sleep, Sam? Sleep or pain?

Charlie wandered in, tail wagging, eyes bright, and rested his head on Sam's lap. Lorraine had brought the German Shepherd home as a pup shortly after they were married, and he was, for all intents and purposes, their child.

"What say you, Charles? Pain or sleep?"

Charlie let out a low whine, followed by a loud bark.

"You know, I had a feeling you might say that."

Sam set the Colt on the table, sliding it away, and opened the prescription bottle, washing one of the light green pills down with a mouthful of cold coffee.

He patted the dog on the head.

"Couldn't very well leave you on your own, now could I? You're the only one in this town worth a damn."

Charlie barked, as if to affirm this.

"Vain too. Oh my." Sam stood. "Come on. Let's get our walk in before work."

The morning met them with its usual stirrings as they crossed the lawn and headed south down King Street; the sound of car engines turning over, the wafting scents of coffee and breakfasts mingling with the perfumed, seminal smell of fresh blossoms, the calls of harried mothers summoning their children. Sam let his mind wander, Charlie running ahead.

He'd stayed on as Sheriff after Lorraine passed—for a time, anyway. He realized now he hadn't truly begun to accept her death until nearly a year after they'd put her in the ground. Those last few months on the job had been his misguided attempt at clinging to normalcy; a palliative charade. He couldn't go more than a day without visiting her grave. Even in the frigid dead of winter, he'd be there with fresh daisies like a perpetually stood up prom date.

Only one person had ever questioned him as to his purpose in tending his wife's grave so diligently. Earl Buxton had taunted him one night while being hauled out of Brockton's for a drunk and disorderly.

"Minding the flowers for when your wife wakes up, Sam?" he'd slurred through a dumb grin.

Sam had broken the man's jaw with the butt of a flashlight.

At least a dozen people saw it happen, but they'd all heard what was said as well. No one ever brought it up, and when Buxton started to make noises about pressing charges, a group of his fellow dockworkers made it clear they'd see him run out of town before that happened.

To say Sam was well liked would be an understatement. He'd always been fair, level headed, and even tempered—or at least he had been, before.

He resigned after the incident with Buxton even though no one had asked him to. The job passed to his friend Walt Hardiman, a good man and a more than capable replacement.

Sam took some time for himself after that, though it seemed he was never left alone for long. The town wouldn't let him go that easy. Someone was always dropping in to say hello, to see if he'd come to dinner, if there was anything they could do—to make sure he hadn't blown his brains out or hung himself from the garage rafters.

"Hi Mr. Peters," a small voice sounded from far off.

Sam looked up to find Tommy Richards petting Charlie, the Shepherd giving the boy sloppy licks on the cheek.

"Out early this morning, Tommy," Sam said. "You know when I was your age we didn't exactly rush to school. Doesn't your bus come around nine?"

"It's our last day," the boy said, shifting his backpack and wincing slightly.

Sam could make out the faint ghosts of bruises on his neck and shoulders.

"How are things at home, Tommy?"

"Fine," the boy replied, somewhat automatically.

"How's your mom? I haven't seen her lately."

"She's okay. Daddy likes her to stay home."

"And how's he doing?"

"Good," Tommy answered, his voice flat, atonal; a voice no one should have, never mind a child of eight.

"Remind me, where's he working these days?"

"He says he's looking."

"Right," Sam said, shifting his weight from one leg to the other anxiously. "Well, you go on now, Tommy. I'll see you later."

"Bye." The boy smiled, gave Charlie a last pat on the head, and was off.

Sam whistled, cocking his head back the way they'd come.

"Come on, Charlie. Have to cut our walk short this morning."

Sam drove down the sweeping hill of Dive Street, hugging the white line as overgrown brush lashed the side of the truck, the wind blowing his shaggy hair. The smell of sea salt thickened as he neared downtown. He took a left onto Main, driving slowly past the old brownstone on the corner. Coming from the south it was usually the first building people saw on the way into Graves Harbor, before South Cove Bridge dropped them into the bustling heart of town.

It was where Lorraine's antique shop used to be.

She'd pulled in fair business, making a good enough go in the warmer months to carry on through the slow winters. Tourist trade mostly, but every once in a while she'd had dealings with serious collectors. She'd had a natural eye for detail.

Main was quiet for a weekday morning, and he pulled the truck down behind the pharmacy into the little back lot overlooking the harbor. He sat for a few minutes, listening to the engine click and settle and the gulls crying overhead, aloft on the breeze. The day was warming up and he took his breaker off as he stepped from the truck and made his way around to the street.

Pete Morgan sat on a bench in front of the general store, his ruddy, aged face flushed in the morning light.

"Morning, Pete."

"Sam, good morning. Say, how you been keeping?"

"Pretty fair. And yourself? How's the arthritis these days?" The old man laughed. "Medication's helping a bit. Not much, but what are you gonna do. 'Least I'm still vertical."

Sam smiled and motioned to the store. "I'm heading in, can I grab anything for you?"

Pete shook his head. "Just taking a breather on my walk."

"All right," Sam said, ducking into the shop.

"God in Heaven," Monique Andrews exclaimed as he entered. "Sam Peters, as I live and breathe. Someone take a picture, quick. We need proof he was here." She came around the counter and hugged him. "You know, I hear the kids are daring one another to stand on your porch at night."

"Very funny."

"Dear God, just look at you," she said, stepping back. She turned and took a pack of disposable razors from the counter. "Here," she grinned, "on the house."

He ran his fingers over the beard he'd let come in out of laziness.

"Message received."

"Listen, why don't you come over for dinner sometime this week? It would be great to catch up, and Lord knows

Hank needs an excuse to stay coherent past three in the afternoon."

"I'd like to," he lied, averting his gaze slightly. "It's just the busy season with work. You know how it is."

She put a reassuring hand on his shoulder.

"Honey, the offer is always on the table."

He picked up a Coke and a pack of D batteries for his work radio, paid and left.

Pete had gone, but Sam could make out his shape a few blocks down Main, moving at a steady clip. Sam took a sip of Coke and decided to take a short walk himself, heading across the road.

Jackson Coombs was bent over an engine in his garage, a half smoked butt hanging out of his mouth. He looked up to see Sam walking by.

"Sam," he called, coming over. "How the hell you been?"

"Fair, Jackson," he said, accepting the man's oil stained hand.

"Oh shit, sorry."

"Don't worry about it. So, how's tricks?"

"Business as usual really," he said, removing a well worn Red Sox cap and wiping his brow.

"And how's Andrea?"

Jackson was quiet for a moment, looking down. "She left a couple months back to stay with her parents in Boston. Wasn't working out."

"I'm sorry to hear that."

Jackson sighed, crushing his cigarette underfoot. "Probably for the best. Anyway, I should get back to work. It's good to see you, Sam. Should get together sometime, knock back a few."

"Yeah," Sam nodded. "That sounds fine."

They parted, Sam continuing up Main.

He stopped as he neared the church, however. Reverend Thomson was out doing lawn work. Sam hadn't seen him since the funeral, and he didn't feel like having that particular conversation just then. He turned and headed back toward his truck.

Sam saw Hardiman as he pulled into the station parking lot.

"Hey Peters," Walt called, walking over to the truck as Sam stepped out. "Want your job back? Cause let me tell you, you can have it."

Sam laughed. "Not for all the gold in Fort Knox."

They shook hands.

"But seriously, it's real good to see you."

"You too," Sam replied. "I just wish it could be under better circumstances."

"Why? What's up?"

Sam pushed his hands into his front pockets.

"I'm pretty sure Zeke Richards has been beating on his kid, his wife too most likely. I think it's been going on a while now. Tommy's got visible bruises."

Walt nodded. "I wouldn't put it past him. Zeke's a mean drunk, that's for damn sure."

"Have Social Services look into it, yeah?"

"I'll put in a call today for sure. Headed out to Harry Colson's place right now. Found some dead deer on his property this morning."

"Coyotes? They're around this time of year."

"Naw. They'd be all tore up if it was coyotes. Harry said he found them in one piece. Might be illness among the population. I'm meeting someone there from Animal Control."

"I'm late for work anyway," Sam said, turning back to his truck. "See you, Walt. My love to Margaret and the kids."

"Will do," Hardiman said, tipping his hat.

He pushed the Chevy up the steep hill toward Lenchner's place on the northwest side of town. It was a twisting one lane road, over which the trees had grown wildly for many years, the oppressive canopy lending it the semblance of a dark tunnel. Nearing its end, one had to undo an old chain strung between oaks to continue on. Sam stepped out of the truck and cast its rusted length to the grassy shoulder.

He could understand now why a man might prefer solitude to the bustle of town life; the mindless gossip, the petty grudges, the drudge of routine. He could take it or leave it himself.

He hopped back in the truck and put it in gear, continuing on up the shadowed incline.

No matter how many times he pulled into that sun-drenched yard the majesty of the scene never seemed to diminish. There were many fine New England houses along the coast—farther south they turned into awful, garish

McMansions—but nothing could match the Lenchner house in its archaic grandeur.

It was gothic in style—high gabled, its portico entrance rounded by Corinthian columns—commissioned by a family of wealthy ship builders around the turn of the century. The old salt-silvered shingling had been replaced with gray clapboard when Lenchner first moved in, giving the place a clean, austere look.

The grounds were immaculately kept; Sam's own handiwork. He'd started his landscaping and snowplowing business shortly after leaving the department. The work was steady, and he found being outdoors did him good.

Today's schedule included the usual maintenance—trimming back the hedges, mowing the lawn, weeding and watering the back garden. He was also to lay fresh mulch beneath the bushes surrounding the house.

Whom the old man was keeping the place up for was unknown to Sam. As far as he could tell, Lenchner never had any visitors. In fact, Sam had never laid eyes on the old hermit himself. Yes, there'd been the occasional glimpse of movement in the high windows, a flash of shadow, a boney hand pulling back a curtain—but nothing more.

The local youth had come up with all sorts of grotesque lore about the man, about the house, and just what he got up to in there; the runnings of youthful, overactive imaginations no doubt. But still, such talk circulated amongst even the oldest of town residents.

Secrets, like wounds, fester and run if not properly attended. This goes double for small towns.

It was eleven o'clock as Sam pulled on his gloves, tuned the portable radio to a local rock station, and set to work, the sun warm on his face.

Lenchner stared out from a high third-floor window, gazing down on the yard and beyond it out over the town.

It was as fine a place to wait out his days as any, he supposed. He'd seen too much of the world in his time; become a touch too familiar with its secrets.

He'd come through it though.

He could count himself among the living, if not the blessed ignorant.

Music sounded below, from the landscaper's radio; something about a black hole sun.

A shiver ran through him at the thought.

It was an hour past sunset as Earl cracked into his seventh beer.

The events of the previous night had shaken him badly, though he'd not seen all that Cal had. It was only as they sped back into the harbor, the throttle opened up full, that Cal had told him about the bodies.

Bled out, white and shriveled, heaped upon one another, throats torn out.

Yet he'd seen no blood. Only a few stray droplets marked the deck.

They'd been too afraid to call the authorities, with no reasonable excuse to be on the water at such an hour.

Earl settled back into his crummy old recliner, downing half a can of Coors as the opening sequence of *Duck Dynasty* appeared on the television.

He would drink until it seemed no more than a bad dream.

Just as he'd begun to put it out of mind, a soft rapping

sounded from the front door.

"Son of a bitch," he muttered under his breath. "Piss off, will you? I ain't buying."

The rapping sounded again.

"If that's a goddamn Bible slinger I'm gonna introduce you to God if you don't piss off!"

The rapping ceased, and just as Earl was turning his attention back to the television set, a burst of loud knocks sounded.

"That's it. You're fucking dead, buddy!" Earl shouted, rushing to the door in his boxers and stained wife-beater.

He peered through the peep hole, spying nothing but the empty lane outside.

He threw open the door, and where there'd been empty air only a second before there now stood a tall figure in a black pea coat, a wide brimmed fedora pulled down over his eyes. Behind him, on the porch, sat at least a hundred sparrows; silent, unstirring, watching.

"Who—who the fuck are you?" Earl demanded.

"It matters not," the figure spoke, his breath pluming an unnatural frozen white against the balmy night air. "But you, you're that nice fellow from the boat last night."

A cold sweat broke out on Earl's neck. "You saw us?"

"Us? Oh, you mean your friend Cal. I've just come from his house. He proved immune to my charms, I'm sorry to say. And until I can procure someone more intellectually able, it seems I'll have to make do with you, Earl Buxton." The figure raised his head, revealing gleaming black, bottomless eyes.

Earl's bladder let go, piss soaking through his boxers,

running down his legs.

"Oh my," Jacobi laughed. "Don't worry, Earl. It's happened to far better men than you."

Earl swayed on his feet, drool running down his chin.

"Now invite me in."

"Won't you please come in?" he half-whispered.

Once past the threshold, Jacobi shut the door. He then turned and lifted Earl into the air by his throat, the man rousing from his trance, gagging and struggling.

"Let me be blunt," Jacobi spoke quietly, tracing the soft flesh of Earl's belly with a blade. "I'm about to offer you more than anyone has in your entire pathetic life. Now, while you must accept this gift of your own free will, know this: if you test me, the last thing you will see on earth is your bowels spilling all over this cheap carpet."

Earl whimpered.

"We have an understanding then?"

The man nodded.

"A wise decision, Earl. You won't regret it."

Jacobi's lips pulled back to reveal a mouth full of jagged teeth, crowded in rows like a shark's. They parted, running with off-white fluid, and Earl lost consciousness.

"Thanks for coming down, Sam," Hardiman said, placing a hand on the man's shoulder. "I'm sorry to ask, but I need an extra pair of steady hands right now."

"Jesus, Walt, you're white as a sheet. What the hell is going on? Parker didn't tell me much on the phone."

"It's Cal Norris," Walt said, gesturing over his shoulder with a flashlight. Sam followed him past the patrol cars and around the side yard of the house where Deputy Jim Parker was bent double over a patch of vomit stained grass. Walt gave the man a pat on the back as they passed.

"Mattie was hysterical when we got here. The paramedics had to sedate her."

They walked through the gated fence into the backyard. The back deck lights had been turned on, illuminating the sloping lawn.

Ahead, Cal Norris sat in a lawn chair, his back to the house, facing out toward the woods that abutted the yard. They walked around front of him, Hardiman raising the flashlight beam to reveal the man's face.

Sam had dealt with bodies during his time with the Graves Harbor police. He'd seen more than his fair share of car wrecks; people torn in half, burned, bodies all smashed to hell and gone. There was the sprinkling of suicides that occurred in every community over the years. Then there'd been the boat accident in the summer of 2012. Drunk tourist kids who forgot whose turn it was to steer the speedboat. They'd crashed head on into the breakwater, half naked bodies flung through the air at forty miles an hour, coming down on solid rock. Four died, one had the good sense to jump out of the boat at the last second, and one was a permanent vegetable, taking meals through a tube. More than that, he'd seen the most beautiful woman he'd ever known waste away before him like an animal in a trap, desperate to live.

But it all paled in comparison to this.

Cheeks slit open from ear to ear in a hideous grin, nose sliced off, eyes cut out—wildflowers bloomed from the empty sockets. Cal's heart had been removed and placed in his bound, swollen hands. A few flies lifted from his face on the night breeze, only to light on it again.

"God almighty," Sam whispered.

"Doubt God's got anything to do with it."

"No one's touched or moved him?"

Hardiman shook his head. "No one's even gone near him."

"Good. You need to get the medical examiner down here while this is all fresh. And alert the State Police."

"Already put in the call," Walt nodded.

They stood for a moment, neither of them speaking.

"Who the hell could have done this, Walt?"

"Damned if I know," he replied, "but whoever it is, I've got a bad feeling they aren't finished yet."

He led Sam back toward the house to where a spotlight had been set up against a section of siding.

In a bloody, swirling script were the words:

The woods are lovely, dark and deep,
But I have promises to keep,
And miles to go before I sleep,
And miles to go before I sleep.

Both men turned back to Cal Norris, who stared without eyes into the shadowed wood beyond.

Earl awoke freezing, pouring sweat. His skin felt as if it were running with insects, itching unceasingly. His blood pumped like fire, his innards writhing. He rolled over onto his stomach and lifted his head to the glow of the television screen. The colors were all wrong. They had inverted, each hue presenting its polar opposite like in some hellish cartoon. But it wasn't just the television. Similar effects were washing over his entire field of vision, the room breathing and shifting, surfaces rippling.

"Don't fight it, Earl," spoke Jacobi from the couch, where he sat perusing an issue of *Hustler* magazine. "You'll just make it harder on yourself." He smiled and held up the centerfold for Earl to see—a cream-skinned redhead spread-eagled on a white sand beach. "You know, in my day women were much more modest. Coverings leave more to the imagination, don't you agree?"

Earl moaned from the floor.

"But then I suppose you don't have much of an imagination, do you Earl? You drink too much. I can taste it." Jacobi chuckled to himself, tossing the magazine to the floor. "'Oh that men should put an enemy in their mouths to steal away their brains!' I don't suppose you're a fan of Shakespeare, Earl?"

Earl vomited on the carpet.

Everything was so sickeningly heightened, his head awash with sensation; drowning in a tactile ocean. His ears rung with dins both near and far. Smells flooded his sinuses; mold, stale pizza, curdled milk, his own stench—a heady mingling of urine, feces, and sweat—all vying for dominance. The gritting of his teeth crackled like fireworks in his skull.

"I met Shakespeare once," Jacobi continued, reminiscent, "strolling in the royal gardens on a midsummer's eve following one of his court performances. He nearly caught me feeding on a page." He laughed, removing his pocket watch to check the time.

To Earl its ticking sounded like cannon fire.

"Shouldn't be much longer, my good man. Soon you'll feel bright and shiny and new, and you'll be able to start your work. There is much to be done, Earl." Jacobi stood, adjusting his coat. "But first I must indulge my sweet tooth."

Lenchner hardly slept, and the little rest he did get was always during the daylight hours. Old habits died hard, and try as he might, he could never close his eyes past sundown. There were too many noises in the night, and too many shadows in which to lurk.

They couldn't enter on their own; the fictions had that part right. And they could not abide the sun. But these rules did not apply to their familiars, those half-turned daylight slaves.

How many had he killed over the years? It seemed a different life now.

He could still remember his first. After the war, when they'd been fleeing Eastern Europe like rats. It happened in Warsaw, which, at the time, was little more than a smoldering, skeletal ruin. A youngling, newly turned, had been stalking the southern district, gorging itself on victims of the burgeoning sex trade. It had taken him several weeks to study its feeding patterns and trace it to the bombed out department store where it was nesting. It had been sleeping in a cistern.

The look on its face as he raised the stake over its chest had not lessened the pain he felt, but it did bring back the faces of his parents, of Rachel, smiling upon him as he rammed the sharpened wood home and the monster's wide, panic-stricken eyes sank back in its skull, its body collapsing with the papery, ripping crackle of a late-season beehive.

He'd sworn to kill them all, and believed he'd come close to it.

He'd not encountered a Master in close to forty years, and younglings never survived long without their makers, unable to transmit the disease until maturation.

Even if he was wrong, their numbers would be low. They were not fitted to the modern world, and there were other slayers yet to carry on his work.

His heart wasn't as strong it used to be, so the doctors had said, and though the idleness of retirement did not suit him, it was wise to exercise caution. He was still the keeper of that which must be kept, the hider of that which must be hidden.

The old man remained vigilant.

Comic books and toys strewn on the floor before him, Tommy Richards rocked slightly, arms about his legs, knees tucked under his chin. The sounds of profanity and crashing objects pervaded the house as his father raged in the living room.

The boy worried for his mother more than himself, for she drew the brunt of his father's ire, cold and merciless as it was. But still, on the nights she passed out early, having drunk herself into a stupor, the old man would come scratching around his door, belligerent and looking for something to hurt—or worse.

He chose a Batman comic, flipping through its pages, trying in vain to distract himself from the tumult at the other end of the house.

It was always there, staring him in the face; a simple truth. The truth that, sooner or later, his father was going to kill both him and his mother.

He'd promised as much, more times than Tommy could

recall. And while promises made in blackout states seldom came to fruition, this one—quietly and adamantly repeated over the years—had taken on a certain air of inevitability. In a while, when he was sure his father had passed out or left the house, he would tiptoe out to make sure his mother was still breathing. He would then go about his nightly ritual. First he would prop a chair against his bedroom door—he never expected it to actually hold anyone back, but perhaps to slow them down, and make a lot of noise in the process. He would set a coffee can containing three years worth of allowance on his nightstand, where it could be reached easily in a hurry. He would open the window halfway, and then crawl beneath untucked sheets with his clothes still on. Finally, he would pray.

He was stirred from his thoughts by a scratching sound at the window. He turned, and as he did so an awful white face swam up to the glass like a monstrous fish from terrible depths; something that had never known the sun's warmth. It smiled, and with an equally pale hand motioned for him to approach.

To his surprise, Tommy felt himself obeying, standing and moving toward the window, unlatching and sliding it open.

"Good evening, young master," the figure spoke, bowing. "Allow me to introduce myself. I am Karl Nicholaus Jacobi, of the Königsberg Jacobis. And what, may I ask, is your name?"

"Tommy Richards," the boy spoke, eyes wide and glazed, pupils dilated.

"Well, young master Thomas, I've been watching you, and I couldn't help but notice—"

"What is Kern-igs-borg?" Tommy interrupted, swaying on

his feet a little.

Jacobi's grip tightened on the window frame, splintering the wood.

"Kön-igs-berg. It is a city. They call it by a different name now. But that doesn't matter. What matters, young Thomas, is that I'd like you to come with me."

"Come with you," Tommy repeated, his voice flat.

"Yes," Jacobi whispered, smiling.

The boy was just to his taste—blonde haired, fair skinned—angelic, as he had preferred them in life.

"And soon there will be other children for you to play with. We can start a new family."

"A new family…"

"That's right," said Jacobi, opening his arms to the boy, fingers spread wide, long, jagged nails like talons. "Now come to me."

And he did.

The old, retired Graves Harbor Elementary School had sat in disrepair for over eleven years, stuck in bureaucratic limbo while town fathers debated whether to sell the property or restore the building as municipal offices.

And so the old red brick building had continued upright, unattended and near forgotten, the grounds going to seed. Emptied classrooms, their desks and chairs long since cannibalized by the other district schools, grew rank with mold and rot. At night the faint echoes of childish voices still whispered its shadowed halls. The black top parking lot was no more than a graveyard of shells dropped by the harbor gulls. The ground floor windows had been boarded up following a spate of vandalism several years back, and reports that vagrants had been sheltering there.

Earl parked his truck on Arbor Street and walked the three blocks along a disused trail skirting Old Pond around back of the school so as not to draw attention.

He was reborn. It felt to him as though his mind had been pulled out of his former wasted, bloated shame of a body and set in one thirty years younger; and more than that, thirty times stronger. The sickness, the fevered sensory overload of hours earlier had smoothed out into a heightened, preternatural awareness. Though it was still dark, he could see everything with perfect clarity, the world before him blanketed in ethereal, glowing auras. The night was alive. An owl on a tree branch thirty yards off was as clear and detailed to his eye as the ground beneath his feet. He could see the individual stains on its plumage, the milky coverlet of its wide, predatory eyes.

He too had hunter's eyes now.

He whistled softly as he began to pry the boards from a small window on the ground floor, in an alcove where dumpsters had once sat. With his newfound strength the task was completed in mere seconds, Earl pulling himself up into the building.

He had worked as a janitor there in the years before the school closed, at least before he'd been fired for drinking on the job. Still, he remembered the layout of the building well.

Passing the main office, he took the central stair down to the sub-basement, walking by what used to be the old art studio and a room which had served as an office for the special education staff.

The basement storeroom next to the boiler was light-tight, he remembered, and he imagined it would serve them well. He would clean it out and install a lock from the inside.

He would prove his worth, and when the Master arrived he would be rewarded for his service. This Jacobi had promised him; this and so much more.

He would taste of the Master's blood.

His nighted baptism.

Returning home from his errand, the gray murk of sunrise collecting in the east as he stepped into the darkened house, Earl could hear soft whimpering from the back bedroom. He moved into the hallway. The light from the bedside lamp flickered as a figure passed by it with a flittering quickness, the pale, lank form of Jacobi stepping into the hall. He grinned, naked and panting, a sheen of sweat glistening his forehead.

"Good morrow, Earl. I take it you've had a productive evening?"

Earl craned his head to look past him into the bedroom. He could see the nude backside of a child, hands tied to the knobs of the headboard with metal wire.

"I asked you a question, Earl," Jacobi pressed, but to no response. He turned to the bedroom and then back to the silent man.

"Oh," he laughed, "Tommy and I were just having some fun. Would you fancy a go, Earl? I think he's still got a little fight in him."

"Tommy Richards is missing and someone just carved Cal Norris up like Jack the fuckin' Ripper. Now I pray to God those two things aren't related, but either way I'm still up shit creek without a paddle here," Hardiman spoke, raising a cup of coffee to his lips. "I need all the help I can get, Sam."

Sam ran a hand through his shaggy hair, shaking his head.

"Walt, I'm sure you can—"

"I'm asking you as a friend, Sam. I need you. Like it or not you've still got your finger on the pulse of this town. You know it better than anyone."

Sam took a deep breath.

Lorraine wouldn't have let him walk away from this. She would never have let him live it down.

"All right, Walt. Let's not waste any time then. Cal's gone, God rest his soul, so that makes Tommy our priority. Put an Amber Alert out and bring in Zeke and Sue for interviews. Split them up, and get a Domestic Abuse counselor in to speak with Sue. Make sure she knows we can provide protection for her if Zeke's done something stupid. Find out if there was any drama—worse than usual drama—just before Tommy disappeared. He could have just run off. Could be hiding in the woods or at a friend's place. We'll need volunteers for sweeps of the woods—"

Hardiman's desk phone rang and he picked it up.

"Hardiman, and this better be damn good." He sat listening for a long minute as Sam looked on. "Right," he said finally. "I'll be down there in fifteen. Yes. Thank you, Pete." He hung up.

"Who was it?"

"Pete Morgan. He found a boat run aground off Lookout Point on his morning walk."

"So call the Coast Guard. We need all hands on deck—"

"It's full of bodies, Sam."

Brian O'Connor sipped at a cheap cup of coffee as he drove south on 95 out of Providence.

He could have let one of the younger guys take the case, but when he heard the details he'd wanted it. Work had been slow as of late, and he had to keep moving.

That was how it caught you; when you slowed down.

By outward appearance the thirty-nine year old seemed healthy and robust, but the inside was a different matter entirely. The cancer that started in his pancreas had put its black tendrils out into his liver and up into his lungs. When the doctor told him he had a year at best he'd told the man to go fuck himself. He'd not been back to the hospital since. That was nearly two years earlier.

If he could just keep moving, he could keep it out of mind.

Focus was everything, and now he had a new one.

Murder in Graves Harbor.

He'd left everything else behind, in a strange country, in a different world, in another life. He'd shut Jen out so she would leave, so she would take Jake with her. He'd cut off old friends. He'd moved into a small apartment, which he only occasionally slept in. When he wasn't working he walked the streets. He couldn't stand the quiet; figured there would be more than enough of it before long.

As he drove now, his thoughts were on the particulars of the case. Cal Norris, forty-three, married, no children, found on the night of June thirteenth in back of his home. Deep facial lacerations, heart removed and placed in hands in a highly ritualized fashion. A message had been found near the scene composed in the victim's blood. Lines from a Frost poem.

It didn't matter so much what particulars of the message were. They always said the same thing.

Hi. I exist. I know you exist. Come find me.

And he would. He had. Many times before.

Too many, perhaps.

But he was good at it. And that was too rare a thing in the world to walk away from.

Still, this one was brazen, and intelligent at that.

This one wouldn't make many mistakes.

All the better.

He smiled to himself as he drove on.

"I've never seen anything like that in my life," Pete Morgan spoke, looking past Walt and Sam out toward the beached vessel. "Throats torn out like some animal got to 'em. But no blood. What could do that?"

"Not sure, Pete. But don't you worry yourself about it. That's our job," Sam said, putting a hand on the shaken man's shoulder. "Why don't you head on home and try to settle down. Fix yourself a drink maybe. We can get a statement later."

Pete nodded. "Yeah. Think that's just what I'll do."

"I'll give you a lift," Walt said.

"No. I think I'd rather walk, if that's all right. It'll help clear my head."

"You sure?"

The man nodded.

"Oh and one more thing, Pete," Sam added. "If you could keep this quiet just for now, I'd really appreciate it. Don't want to spook anyone."

"Too late for that," he said.

They watched him set off down the beach.

Walt turned to Sam. "All this in twenty-four hours? It's more than you're liable to see in twenty-four years."

"I know it."

Sam's cell phone rang and he answered it.

"Hello?"

"Mr. Peters, this is Friedrich Lenchner. When can I expect you at the house today?"

"I'm afraid I won't be able to make it, Mr. Lenchner. There's been a string of crimes in the last twenty-four hours, including a murder. I've been deputized by Sheriff Hardiman to help assist."

The line went quiet.

"Mr. Lenchner?"

Silence.

"Mr. Lenchner, are you there?"

"Yes... I'm sorry to have detained you... I was unaware."

"Is everything all right, Mr. Lenchner?"

"Fine. Everything is fine. I will let you go. Good day."

"Good day."

Sam flipped the cell closed, sliding it back into his pocket.

"What was that?" Walt asked.

"It's nothing."

Lenchner flipped on the digital radio scanner he'd purchased ten years earlier and tuned in the local police frequencies.

A homicide. Possibly multiple homicides. A child missing.

The most that had ever gone afoul in Graves Harbor since he'd lived there—in one night.

He paced his study, his silver serpent-headed cane tapping on the hardwood floor as he went.

Keep your wits about you, old fool.

Don't jump to conclusions. It could be nothing.

But his intuition told him otherwise.

If it was indeed one of them, it was sloppy work. And they didn't do sloppy. Never did. Couldn't afford to.

This was purposeful; a message.

This was a vampire announcing itself.

Announcing itself to him.

"Could human teeth do this? Sure they could. Would have to be one snaggletoothed bastard though," John Dupree, the medical examiner, spoke, hovering over one of the corpses with a clipboard. "But here's what throws me off—these men are almost totally exsanguinated, with barely a drop spilt."

"So what are we talking about here?" Hardiman asked.

Dupree shook his head. "Damned if I know. Something I sure as hell haven't seen before."

The evening sun hung low in the west, going down in a fury of scarlet-vermillion.

"I'd like to get these boys back to the lab so I can examine them more thoroughly, if you gentlemen will excuse me."

"You'll be sure to let us know straight away if you find anything of interest," Sam said, Dupree giving an affirmative wave of the hand as he headed off.

Another man was walking toward them from the parking lot.

"Sheriff Hardiman?"

"That's me," Walt answered.

"Brian O'Connor, State Homicide. Deputy Parker said I could find you here," he said, extending his hand.

Walt shook it.

"Glad to have you." He motioned to Sam. "Detective, this is Sam Peters, former Sheriff of Graves Harbor. I've asked him to come on as a deputy until we get this mess sorted."

"Good to meet you," O'Connor said, shaking Sam's hand.

"Likewise."

"So what have we got here?" O'Connor asked, looking toward the ship.

"Ten dead Romanian fishermen who seem to have gotten very lost."

"Is this at all related to Cal Norris's murder?"

"No idea. We're waiting on a more thorough report from the medical examiner. As I'm sure you've already guessed, Detective, we're in uncharted waters here."

"Aren't we all," O'Connor replied. "Well, to start I could use a place to get organized, if you can spare it."

"We can clear you an office at the station." Sam turned to Hardiman. "Walt, why don't you take the detective back and get him situated. I'll see things finished here."

Hardiman nodded. "You sure you've got it?"

"I'm sure. Now go on. Tell two of the men to double up and leave a cruiser for me."

"Will do," Hardiman said, heading toward the Point parking lot with O'Connor at his side.

Sam walked the beach as they began to load the bodies

into the examiner's van.

Grace had been waiting for this night, having succumbed to that uniquely nervous strain of expectation—that of the virginal. But now that it was upon her, she suddenly felt unsure of herself.

She'd been seeing Devon Sonders going on three months. He was intent upon this night, and she felt resigned to it despite her creeping apprehension.

This wasn't how she'd imagined it being.

The back of an SUV, smelling of sweaty football gear and old takeout, parked on the wooded outskirts of town. He— grunting and sweating over her like a beast, stinking of cheap gin, pushing her face down into the seat, his mask of pleasantries having slipped entirely.

"Stupid bitch," he spat, breath hot against her ear. "You like that, you fucking slut? I bet you fucking love it."

"OK stop," she said, trying to sit up.

"What?" he asked, incredulous.

"I said stop, get off me."

He pushed her back down. "I'm not done with you yet."

"I don't care. I don't want this," she said, beginning to struggle, though no match for his strength.

"You fucking tease." He thrusted harder now, wrapping a hand around her throat. "I'm gonna make you fucking want it."

Seeing that resistance was useless, she closed her eyes, hoping that he would finish quick. But he was drunk and having trouble finding his stroke, banging away at her like a savage.

At some point she heard the sound of a door being opened, and Devon's confused voice.

"Hey, what the—"

She opened her eyes to see him pulled off her, out of the car and thrown through the air with tremendous force, flying face first into an oak.

She lay stunned for a moment, before sitting up and peering out the door at Devon's crumpled form. Blood and brain matter leaked from his broken skull.

"Dev?" she whispered meekly.

"Well don't be rude, Devon," Jacobi spoke, picking up the boy's broken body by the neck and walking it over to the SUV. "Answer the poor girl. Can't you see she's startled?" He moved Devon's mouth, bloody, shattered bits of tooth falling out as he ventriloquised in a high falsetto. "*Hello Grace! I'm sorry I hurt you, but it's the only way I can get it up! Diddly-deeeeeeeeee!*"

He dropped the dead boy to the leaf strewn ground and spat on him, turning his attention to Grace.

"My dear, just look at the state of you. Here, allow me." Jacobi removed his coat, wrapping it about her. "There. No one is going to hurt you." He tipped her face up to his with a long white finger, and what she saw in the black deeps of his eyes washed away all apprehension, all fear. She went limp in his arms, Jacobi lifting her, sweeping her off into the night.

Sam was about to head back to the station when he noticed a dark form moving up the beach. He switched on his flashlight, shining it at the figure.

"Who is that? Identify yourself."

"Would you please not shine that in my face, Mr. Peters," an old voice spoke.

"Mr. Lenchner?"

"Yes."

Sam could see the man's face now—gray and wizened.

"This is a crime scene, Mr. Lenchner. You can't be out here."

Lenchner was silent, looking past Sam toward the beached vessel, now covered in yellow police tape.

"May I ask what happened?"

"Some fishermen were killed."

"How were they killed?"

"I can't discuss that with you, Mr. Lenchner."

"Were their throats torn out?"

Sam hesitated. "How do you know that?"

"And there was almost no blood?"

"How could you know that?"

"A lucky guess," Lenchner said, resting his cane in the crook of his arm.

"Mr. Lenchner, if you know something about this you need to tell—"

"Go home, Mr. Peters, if you know what's good for you. Lock up, close your blinds, and answer the door for no one until dawn."

"What are you talking about, Mr. Lenchner?"

He was walking away.

"The dead ride the night in Graves Harbor, Mr. Peters," Lenchner called over the noise of rolling surf. "Und die Todten reiten schnell."

Sam stood and watched the old man disappear down the beach.

The bar was nearly empty save for old Brockton himself and a few of the usual flies. Roger Kemp, a local lawyer and well known lush, was about halfway through his fourth martini, the olives collected neatly on a napkin beside his pack of Camels. He loosened the checkered noose about his neck and unbuttoned his collar, turning to the man at his elbow.

"I need a new line of work, Patty."

Patty Novak nodded, the image of himself collecting trash at fifty forming in his mind. He knocked back the last of his whiskey and motioned to Brockton for another.

"You go slow, Patty boy," Brockton said, filling the glass and sliding it across the brown lacquered countertop. "I'm not scraping your sorry ass off the floor tonight."

"You ever gonna let me live that down, old timer?"

"Nope. But don't feel bad, Patty boy. I've scraped up just about all the regulars at one point or another. Ain't that right, Roger?"

Kemp laughed and raised his martini. "Righto, skip."

The bar door swung open, and a dark figure stood at the threshold without speaking.

"Come in if you're drinking, friend," Brockton said from the bar, the other men turning.

Jacobi smiled, removing his hat.

"Why thank you."

He entered, locking the door behind him.

Sam and Hardiman sat across the office table from Jim Parker over coffee. The wall clock read *11:25*.

"So I talked with Earl Buxton this morning regarding Cal," Parker spoke. "Said he hadn't seen him in a few days. When I told him what happened he broke down. Said he couldn't imagine who would want to hurt Cal."

"So a dead end in other words," Walt said.

"What about Zeke and Sue? How did the interviews go?" Sam asked.

"Like I imagined they would," Parker sighed. "They came in plastered, hysterical. Couldn't get much sense out of them. Turns out alcoholics don't handle crises very well," he chuckled.

"Is that a fucking joke?" Sam shot back, Parker's smile disappearing.

"Hey, I didn't mean—"

"No, I'm sorry. I'm very tired. I know we all are. But let's try to keep our heads on straight. Now, I want patrols doubled up tonight. Call in whoever you need to."

"Already taken care of," Walt said, pouring a cup of coffee.

"OK, and where are we at on the woods sweeps for Tommy?"

"Got plenty of volunteers. Can't start tonight obviously, but first thing tomorrow for sure."

"All right," Sam said, getting up. "If you guys can hold it down here for the moment, there's someone I have to go see."

The dock creaked under the weight of the forklift as it raised a large wooden crate and began to roll down the ramp to where Novak's van sat, idling.

"A little farther," Novak called, waving the operator on.

"Be careful," Earl instructed.

"What's in here anyway?" the man asked.

Earl was slow on the answer, Kemp stepping in for him.

"It's an antique armoire. Very rare," he spoke around the butt of his Camel.

"What he said," Earl added.

With the crate secured, Kemp laid a hundred bucks on the man and they were off.

"Where to now?" Novak asked as they pulled away from the waterfront. He scratched at a cluster of puffy, discolored wounds on his neck. They ran slightly as he did so.

"The old meadow at the end of Windward Lane," Earl replied. "Jacobi said to meet him there."

He looked in the rearview, back to where Brockton and Kemp sat on opposite sides of the massive crate, running their hands over it.

"It's the Master, isn't it?" Kemp asked.

"He's going to make us gods," Brockton said.

Earl stared on, silent.

They arrived in the meadow just after midnight, but Jacobi was nowhere to be seen. The men got out of the van and looked around.

"Where is he?" Novak asked.

"There," Brockton said, pointing.

Jacobi emerged from the sylvan shadows into the light of the three quarters moon, leading Tommy Richards and Grace Dreger by the hands. Both were naked, save for wreaths of wildflowers set atop their heads, their hands bound with lengths of woven briars.

"Gentlemen," he spoke, "stand the crate here."

They did as they were told, each man taking a corner, and standing it up where Jacobi had indicated.

Jacobi motioned for them to step back.

He approached the crate and knocked on it.

"Shave-and-a-hair-cut."

Two quiet knocks answered from within.

There came the low groan of bending wood and the crate exploded, splinters and sawdust flying in all directions, the men covering their eyes.

When the air cleared, two figures stood amongst what remained of the crate.

One was a young, dark-skinned woman of Indian origin.

Long dark hair framed a face that, though cruel, was possessed of a devastating beauty. Her black eyes, like Jacobi's, were as deep as the waters of the Lethe.

Beside her stood a man of advanced age with stern Anglo-Saxon features; aquiline nose, high cheekbones, brows thick and dark. His ghostly white head was bald save for a few wisps on the very top, and a heavy moustache curled his upper lip.

"Father," Jacobi spoke, bowing. He motioned for the men to do the same. "Gentlemen, allow me to introduce my father, Lement—son of Aigmar, Lord of the hill tribes of Akrar, devourer of men and Maker of the chosen—your Master."

A pack of slinking coyotes emerged from the woods, and began circling about the group at a distance, heads bowed in a show of obedience.

"My son has been busy," Lement spoke, observing the men. "What say you, Mara?"

The woman only had eyes for Grace, tongue running over the curvature of her jagged teeth.

"He has chosen well, Father. As is his nature."

Jacobi pulled the children forward.

"I bring gifts. For my sister, a beautiful youth. Freshly deflowered as it happens."

Mara took Grace from Jacobi, hands greedy about the girl's neck and breasts, sniffing her flesh. Grace shivered, squeezing her eyes closed.

"And for you, Father," Jacobi continued, "the sweetest of pets."

He pushed Tommy to his knees before Lement.

The old vampire leaned down to the boy's face.

"What is your name, child?"

"Tommy," he spoke, trembling, his voice no more than a hushed whisper.

"Tell me," Lement said, "did Mr. Jacobi do anything naughty to you while you were in his custody?"

Tears welled in Tommy's eyes and his gaze turned downward.

Lement looked to Jacobi.

"Karl, you're incorrigible."

Jacobi smiled.

"But boys will be boys, I suppose." Lement turned back to Tommy. "I promise you that mean Mr. Jacobi won't hurt you ever again."

Tommy let out a shallow breath, betraying a small measure of relief.

Lement's eyes gleamed in the dark.

"I'll be the one hurting you from now on."

The boy began to scream.

"That voice, my my. I do believe I'll geld this one."

Sam knocked on Lenchner's door, the night wind moaning in the eaves.

"Mr. Lenchner, it's Sam Peters. I need to speak with you."

No movement sounded within.

"You know something about what's happening, Mr. Lenchner. I'm not leaving until you speak to me."

He heard the creak of footsteps, and the old man opened the door.

"You'd better come in then."

Lenchner led Sam toward the back of the house to a large room that served as a library. Ancient texts lined its walls and lay strewn over a large mahogany desk. An old woodcut hung above the fireplace, an elaborate rendering of Saint George and the Dragon. Sam studied this for a moment.

"What you said to me on the beach, what did you mean by that?"

Lenchner sat in a high-backed chair behind the desk, cane

laid across his lap.

"Are you a religious man, Mr. Peters? Do you believe in forces larger than yourself?"

"I like to think so. I don't see what that has to do with—"

Lenchner raised a hand.

"It has *everything* to do with what's happening here."

He took a leather-bound book from the pile atop the desk, opened it and turned it toward Sam.

"*Les Diaboliques Nocturne*," Sam read.

"Nosferatu, strigoi, jiangshi, vetala, aluka, the walking death; the name doesn't matter, nor the origin. So long as man has existed, they have existed. They *were* men once. Plucked from history and imbued with unnatural power."

"Mr. Lenchner," Sam spoke, exasperated, "I haven't got time for fairy tales. Now, do you want to tell me about the person or persons we're dealing with, or do I have to haul you down to the station for obstruction?"

"I assure you, Mr. Peters—"

He was cut off by the sound of breaking glass from the front of the house.

"Stay here," Sam said, pulling his weapon from its holster and moving down the hall. A rock had shattered a pane of glass in the foyer.

He threw open the door, pistol at the ready, only to be confronted by an old man standing at the bottom of the marble steps.

"Good evening. Samuel Peters is it?"

"Who are you? How do you know me?

The figure looked beyond Sam into the house.

"Are you in there, old slayer? Come out, come out."

Lenchner stepped past Sam into the night air, the silver tip of his cane clicking on the stone.

"Name yourself, monster."

"Lement," the vampire spoke. "I've not had the pleasure, though I do believe you knew the first of my progeny. His name was Lyall. It is a Celtic name derived from the Old Norse word 'Liulfr'—it means 'wolf'."

"I do not recall," Lenchner lied. "None of you are worth remembering."

"Do not test me, slayer," Lement hissed. "You know full well why I've come." The vampire extended a pale hand, sickly long fingers curling into a powerful fist. "You have spilt blood of my blood, rent flesh of my flesh, and stolen what I tasked Lyall to recover. As he lay dying I drank of his essence, and though the echo of the memory was faint, I heard a name resounding there, like something from a waking dream: *Friedrich Lenchner*... Of course you'd fled by that time, and I lost you to the bustle of the masses. But what does an immortal have if not time? I went to ground, I slept, and as the years passed the world grew smaller, the places to hide fewer and farther between. Imagine my surprise upon waking to find you living in the open under your given name, bold as brass." Lement smiled. "The past rules us with a far sterner hand than the future, eh Friedrich? Even with all the smothering uncertainty of the latter." He laughed, capering nimbly along the perimeter of the house. "The dance of the present moves only to the music of the past. A dance in which all steps are utterly familiar, passed down the ages in pain and blood and repetition. You couldn't deny your past, and so here we are."

"What you seek, I destroyed it many years ago," Lencher said. "You're too late."

Lement laughed. "You stink of lies, old slayer. If it could be destroyed, someone would have done so long before you."

Sam raised his gun at Lement.

"Did you kill Cal Norris?"

"No, that was my son. He is short tempered, I admit."

"Where is Tommy Richards?"

"The boy is *mine* now."

"Put your hands in the air and turn around," Sam ordered.

Lement grinned. "Go fuck yourself."

Sam fired, the bullet tearing a hole just above Lement's right knee.

"Fine shot. I rather liked these pants though. Tailor made."

Sam fired again, the bullet opening up below Lement's right shoulder—to no effect.

"I seem to have worn out my welcome," he sighed, bowing. "Guten abend, Herr Lenchner, Herr Peters. Until another."

Lement melted into shadow and out of sight.

"Do you believe me now?" Lenchner asked, walking back into the house.

Sam stared into the darkness, unspeaking.

The sun rose on Graves Harbor in all its golden brilliance, another night passed into the histories.

In his church, Reverend Thomson swept up and down the rows, placing new programs into the pew shelves. He'd opened the front doors to air out the hall, and the whisper of a light breeze accompanied him as he whistled "I'll Fly Away" to himself.

A shadow rose down the center aisle, Thomson looking up to see who it was.

Against the sunlight he could not make out the man's face, but he greeted him none the less.

"Good morning, friend. I'm just cleaning up a bit, but please feel free to come in. The Lord's house is always open."

"Not anymore," the figure spoke, raising something in its hands.

"Mr. Buxton? Is that—?"

"The Master sends his regards, holy man."

Earl brought the axe down in a rush of air, the blade connecting with the Reverend's shoulder, sinking in up to the hilt.

Slipping into shock without so much as a whisper, Thomson groped dumbly at the handle, eyes wide, mouth gaping like a fish.

Earl put a boot on the man's chest and pushed, wrenching the blade loose with a spray of arterial blood.

Thomson fell backward onto the burgundy carpet, twitching, a low moan gurgling in his throat. Earl brought the axe down again, this time on the man's sternum, sinking in with a wet crunch. Thomson's eyes began to roll back, but before he lost consciousness Earl pulled the axe free once more, spinning it around to the blunt side and raising it over the man's head.

"*His* will be done," Earl said, and let fall again and again, until all that remained of the Reverend was a wet heap of hammered flesh and splintered bone.

Driving home, Sam recounted the events of the previous night. All he'd seen, all that had transpired, it was too much for his mind to process. He was running on little sleep, though he couldn't imagine sleeping under the present circumstances. He would stop by the house to check on Charlie and pick up a few things, then he had to get back to the station.

They would have to set a curfew.

Supernatural or not, there was a dangerous element in town. He could justify a curfew given the events of the past forty-eight hours. Everyone in their homes before sunset.

No need to mention vampires.

At the house he filled Charlie's dish and refreshed his water, then set about collecting a few items; a box of ammunition for the Colt, and his snub-nosed .38, which he slipped into an ankle holster. In the kitchen he forced down some buttered toast, though he had no appetite. He kept staring across into the dining room where a simple wooden cross hung on the wall; something Lorraine had put up when they'd first moved in. He looked away, but his eyes returned to it again.

"Fuck it."

He walked over and took it off the wall, bringing it with him as he left the house.

Heading past the church downtown, Sam could see an ambulance and several police cars parked in front. He pulled in and was met by a pale, ill looking Walt Hardiman.

"What's going on, Walt?"

"It's the Reverend. He... He..."

"What is it?"

"Someone took an axe to him, Sam. You can barely tell it's him."

"Jesus Christ," Sam said, putting a hand over his face. "Jesus fucking Christ."

Walt leaned in close.

"Laura Dreger just called to report her daughter Grace is missing, and Sam, some bike riders found Devon Sonders on the edge of town this morning, dead of a compound skull fracture."

"We're setting a curfew, Walt, starting tonight. Everyone off the streets before sundown. At least until we get ahead of this thing. Call whoever you have to and make it happen."

Walt nodded.

"And get some sleep once things are set here, ok? We're going to need everyone sharp come nightfall."

O'Connor exited the church and walked over to the car, pulling off a pair of rubber gloves.

"Is it the same bastard who killed Cal?" Sam asked.

O'Connor shook his head. "I'd be surprised if that was the case. Norris's murder was clean, surgical. This is messy." He looked back toward the building. "Very messy—"

BOOM.

The sound of a gun blast cut through the morning air, Walt and O'Connor ducking. Sam turned to look out the back window.

Old Harry Colson was walking down the center of Main, shotgun in hand, eyes wild.

Sam clicked the safety off the Colt as he opened the door and stepped out of the car, keeping the weapon low at his side. He motioned to Colson with his free hand.

"Harry. Just take it easy now, Harry."

"It was them, wasn't it?" the man called, pumping a spent shell from his gun.

"Who do you mean, Harry?"

"THEM!" he shouted, shaking, gripping the gun in a stranglehold. "THEY COME IN THE NIGHT! DANCE ON THE DAMN ROOF! YOU THINK I DON'T HEAR THEM?!"

"I hear them too, Harry," Sam said. "It's not just you. You're not alone."

Colson stopped walking, a smile spreading across his face.

"YOU'RE WRONG, SAM!" He turned the shotgun on himself. "WE'RE *ALL* ALONE!"

"Harry, don't!"

He stuck the barrel in his mouth and pulled the trigger, the top half of his head exploding.

In the cool belly of the elementary school Grace wailed, biting into the leather belt that had been strapped around her head as a gag. She was tied to the boiler by her hands with an old, filthy electrical cord, nude and blood spattered. A whip crack sounded and yet another laceration opened on her back, accompanied by a lusty gasp escaping Mara's lips.

The whip drew back.

CRACK.

Again.

CRACK.

The rhythm mounting.

CRACK. CRACK. CRACK.

The lashing ceased, and Grace could hear the soft padding of bare feet, Mara stepping around in front of her. She too was naked, radiant in the cold light of the electric lantern overhead. She brushed a few sweaty strands of hair out of her face, tucking them back behind a heavily pierced ear.

"Darling, please," she whispered, wrapping a hand around the girl's throat, choking her. "This is just foreplay." She kissed Grace's bloody, chapped lips. "I'm going to hurt you until you forget what it is *not* to hurt."

She spit in Grace's eye, the one that wasn't already swollen shut.

"That's it," she giggled, grabbing a handful of dirty blonde hair and ripping it out. Grace gagged on the belt, squealing with pain.

"Yes," Mara gasped, playing with herself as she took pliers to the girl's breasts, stretching one nipple out until it opened with a crimson gush.

Grace lost consciousness, at least until Mara poured salt over her shredded backside in a wave of white hot agony.

Down an adjacent corridor, Tommy endured perversions that made her suffering seem a reprieve, their cries echoing in the musty dark.

"They will have a nest," Lenchner spoke, running his hand over a map of the town. "We know there are at least two; Master and progeny. There may be others, and they will have accumulated a number of familiars by now."

"Familiars?" Sam asked.

"Half-turned. No longer human but not yet vampire. They require a Master's blood to effect the change."

"So they're like worker bees?"

"Yes. While they have adopted some of the vampire's physical strengths, they may still walk the day and come and go through residences as they wish. They are also quite moody. The infection upends brain chemistry you see, setting neurotransmitters in a state of agitated flux. This results in hypervigilance, impulsive aggression, manic depression, psychosis and insomnia."

"This is just too much," Sam said, shaking his head. "This is a cult of sickos or something, right? That guy was just cranked up on speed or PCP or something. That's why the bullets didn't—"

Lenchner stopped what he was doing and turned to Sam. "Mr. Peters, there was a time when I didn't believe in monsters. Believe me, there was. And then one night my father invited one in out of a storm, and it taught me to believe. It took my family, one by one. At the time I couldn't understand why it let me live, but over the years I came to realize it was mere vanity. You see, where they can afford to, they wish to be known to us. They resent being the stuff of horror fiction and bad dreams. They long to live in the open."

"Say I believe you; this Lement said you have something of his. What is it?"

Lenchner was quiet, seemingly lost in thought.

"Friedrich?'

"It is a relic. An amulet with an inset stone. It came to man during the fourth millennium BC with the emergence of Sumerian culture in Mesopotamia, now modern day Iraq. The histories tell of a dark, nomadic race travelling the land by night, bartering with strange riches. Little is known of its origin before then."

"You're telling me that this is all over some damn trinket? They're killing—"

"It is a means to a long desired end, Sam. The amulet, when held before the rising sun, invokes a power that— assuming the lore is true— will render a vampire invulnerable to the sun. The myth of day-walking made manifest. They would be beyond reckoning."

"So get the thing out of town. Lose yourself somewhere.

Don't tell anyone where you're going."

Lenchner shook his head.

"I'll not run from them. And even if I did, they'll not stop until they've killed or turned everyone in town. They are fiercely territorial."

"All right, so how do we stop them?"

"Tonight we watch," Lenchner said, picking up an elaborately carved stake. "We hone in on the nest, we identify their familiars if possible. And tomorrow, with the sun at our backs, we seek them out. They are weakened during the daylight hours, and we might even catch them sleeping."

Lenchner glanced at Sam's Colt in its holster.

"That a forty-five?"

Sam nodded.

Lenchner opened a drawer and took out a box of shells, sliding them across the desk.

"Silver hollow points. Won't kill them, but they sure as hell won't tickle."

"What about the amulet? You're not just going to leave it here, are you? Won't these 'familiars' come looking for it?"

Lenchner laughed. "Let's pray they're that stupid."

"What is your will?" Earl asked.

Jacobi ignored the man, humming as he made a series of intricate incisions around the border of Sophia Reardon's face. The woman lay dead, propped against a grimy wall like a discarded mannequin. A cluster of hand-traced Thanksgiving turkeys on paper plates hung overhead, goggling mindlessly.

"So hard to get it all off in one piece," Jacobi spoke, taking hold of the woman's scalp and beginning to pull it down over her face, the flesh coming loose with a wet ripping sound. "But practice has made perfect." With a final, controlled yank, he uncovered the gleaming red musculature beneath, stepping back to admire his work. "The only way to improve upon perfection, Earl, is to mutilate it."

"What is your will?" Earl repeated.

"Tonight I want you and Kemp to go to the old man's house. You are looking for an odd piece of jewelry on a gold chain, with a red inset stone. It will be hard to miss."

"What if we run into Peters and the old man?"

Jacobi shook his head. "They will be on the hunt tonight. Let them play their little game. Besides, father wants the old man alive, and this Boy Scout may be of some use to us yet." Jacobi leaned forward out of the shadows then, his black eyes wide. "Now, tell me everything you know about him."

By sunset the doors of Graves Harbor were locked, families shut into their homes, streets quiet save for the sound of the occasional police cruiser rolling by.

Zeke swam up from the black waters of sleep. The doorbell was ringing, and he had the groggy, semi-conscious impression that it had been for some time. He sat up on the couch, swinging his legs over the side and knocking over a three-quarters empty bottle of Karkov vodka.

"Son of a bitch," he swore, cradling his head in his hands. His vision spun and pulsed along with the rhythm of his heart. His mouth tasted like an old carpet, his tongue feeling dry and gritty.

"Sue," he shouted, "get the door."

There was no response, his wife being passed out in the bedroom.

The bell continued its ringing.

"Damnit," Zeke swore, getting up to answer it.

He pulled the door open.

Tommy stood on the front stoop, looking pale and shaken.

"Tommy, my God," Zeke exclaimed, scooping the boy up, tears welling in his eyes. "Thank God. Where have you been? Where you been, huh?" He carried the boy into the house. "Sue, it's Tommy! He's—"

Tommy brought his hands to his father's face, pushing Zeke's eyes in with his thumbs.

"Tommaaaaaaaahhhhhh!"

Zeke spun about the room, trying to detach the boy from his face. He crashed into walls, breaking pictures. A small table knocked over, lamp crashing to the floor, casting the room in shadow. Tommy held fast as Zeke thrashed and screamed, smiling and laughing.

Sue entered the room, rubbing the sleep from her eyes just in time to see Tommy's jaw unhinge like a snake's, lips pulling back over far too many twisted teeth. She dropped to her hands and knees as the boy latched onto Zeke's throat and the man emptied like a wine sack, skin and muscle shriveling to the bone.

Tommy pulled away with a wet smack, licking blood from his dark lips, and turned to Sue. Some of his color was returning, his white skin turning a warm, blushing pink.

"Don't be scared, Mommy," the boy said, moving towards her, his shadow thrown long and twisted on the wall behind. "It's so much better. And no pain. There's no pain, Mommy."

"You're not Tommy," Sue cried. "What have you done with Tommy?"

"I'm still here, Mommy. I'm just a little different."

He showed her his teeth, and was upon her before she could scream.

In her house across town, Laura Dreger stared out the screen door at a silent figure on the lawn. The front light was out, and her eyes had to adjust to the dark as she walked down the stone steps and out into the yard, the night insects sermonizing.

"Grace? Dear God, is that you, honey?"

Grace stood unmoving, her pale, nude form outlined in the orange light of an adjacent streetlamp.

Laura ran to her.

"Oh honey, what happened? Did someone hurt you?"

"Yes," Mara's voice sounded as she stepped out of the shadows, also naked. "But she's learning to like it."

Laura spun around. "Who the *fuck* are you?"

In a flash of movement Mara twisted the woman's head off, holding it aloft, letting its warmth run over her.

Laura Dreger's headless corpse fell to the ground with a dull thud.

Mara turned her blood spattered body to Grace in offering,

and the girl began to clean her with a greedy tongue, lapping steadily; a dark communion.

Sam crouched next to Lenchner in the woods on the perimeter of the property. The old man stared through the mounted scope of an old M1 Carbine, looking toward the house.

"That thing still fire?" Sam asked.

"I keep it in working order," Lenchner replied without turning. "Just keep an eye out for any movement."

"Like that?" Sam whispered, lining his hand up with the drive, Lenchner following with the scope.

Two figures were approaching.

Earl swung a crowbar as he walked while Kemp carried a glass cutter.

"Remember what Jacobi said," Kemp spoke, "the old man's crafty. Keep your head on a swivel."

"Yeah yeah," Earl replied, waving him off. "He's still an old man. You try your James Bond shit if you want. I'm going in the front."

They walked through the yard and up the stone steps to the

door. Earl tried the polished brass handle, the unlocked door clicking open.

"Hey Roger," he said, turning. "Look, I'm Harry fuckin' Houdini."

"Wait—"

Earl pulled the door open, the gun blast hitting him square in the face, blood, bone, and brain matter spraying Kemp. Earl's body slumped backward in a twitching heap.

"Jesus," Kemp shouted, taking cover. After a few quiet minutes he peeked his head around the doorframe to spy a double barreled shotgun mounted to a heavy chair, a drawstring trigger mechanism attached to the door knob. Looking up, he could see a deadfall of free weights suspended above the door itself, a thin tripwire laid across the threshold set to release it.

Kemp turned back to the yard, and it was only then that he saw the shining bear traps hidden beneath grass trimmings in the moon's silver light. They'd made it through them by sheer chance.

"Fuck me."

Earl gurgled from where he'd fallen on the steps, somehow alive, blood bubbling from his ruined face. Kemp pulled the man up and over his shoulder. "Going in the front, huh Earl?" They made their way across the yard stepping carefully around the traps and back down the shadowed drive.

Lenchner pulled back from the rifle scope and turned to Sam.

"I'm slow. I'll stay here in case more come. You follow them to wherever they go."

"And then what?"

"Just watch, don't try anything on your own. We'll regroup in the morning."

Somewhere far off an owl called.

O'Connor laid out the crime scene photos from Cal Norris's house on the desk before him, his eyes drifting from one to the next. Over the man's wounds again and again, studying the position of the body, how it had been displayed. How it was meant to be found.

It was ritualistic. Reenaction. Experience at play.

The Reverend's murder was a finger painting, as was Devon Sonders's; Norris's, on the other hand, was a masterpiece.

The heart had been removed cleanly, indicating someone with surgical knowledge, or at least a well-practiced hand at dissection. A firm grasp of human anatomy.

A list of area doctors would be as fine a place to start as any, and perhaps a glimpse into the local library records with a flag on surgical texts.

His eyes kept returning to a close-up of Norris's face, flowers inserted into the eye sockets.

"Daffodil bulbs instead of balls / Stared from the sockets of the eyes," he spoke, the lines from Eliot echoing in his mind.

Our man is a fan of poetry, he thought, looking over the words of Frost written on the house's white siding in dark blood.

Promises to keep.

"And what are those, my man?"

The desk phone rang and he picked it up.

"O'Connor."

"Detective, this is John Dupree from the Medical Examiner's office. I think I have something for you."

"Yes?"

"The bite marks on the sailors' throats, I've matched them to a shallow set we found on Cal Norris's left shoulder."

"You're certain they're the same?"

"It's the same sicko, no doubt."

"Could you fax a copy of your report to the Graves Harbor PD? I need to run this by a friend at the Bureau."

"Will do."

"Thanks."

He hung up and sat in silence, rocking back in his chair.

So we've got a biter.

The eccentricities failed to interest him anymore. The secretors, the stranglers, the ones who liked to play surgeon; the ones who arranged, the ones who disarranged; the ones who were patient, the ones who weren't. He'd come to know them all.

"Detective!" Jim Parker called from the front of the

station, startling him. "Get up here quick!"

O'Connor sprung to his feet, running down the narrow corridor past the lobby and out the front of the station to where Parker was standing.

"What is—"

"It's Sophia Reardon," Parker spoke, his face deathly pale.

The flayed woman stood impaled on a pike on the station lawn, the raw muscle glistening under the electric glare of the street lights.

O'Connor looked on in silence.

"The place was booby trapped from front to back," Kemp shouted, standing over the twitching form of Earl.

"Remember your place, Roger," Jacobi spoke, staring at the body. He pointed at Earl's face as the blood slowly congealed, the bone and muscle beginning to knit their way over the open cavity. "He's healing. He won't be the same, nearly, but he *is* healing."

"Give him the blood then!"

"The Master's blood must be earned, Roger. All good things to those who wait."

"Did they earn it?" Kemp asked, motioning to Tommy and Grace as they wandered the darkened halls, enamored of their transformations.

"In their own way," Jacobi whispered.

Hearing this, the children turned and graced him with fanged smiles.

"Where is the Master?" Novak asked, Brockton standing

beside him.

Jacobi turned. "He is about his work."

Just as Sam had seen the men enter the old Elementary School he became aware of a strange phenomenon. There rose, softly at first, a growing choral drone of night insects. He thought little of it initially, concentrating on the school. But as the sound grew, waxing in its complexity with the addition of every new chirp and click, he began to grow uneasy. He covered his ears, the noise, surging to a hideous cacophony, such that he prayed his ear drums might burst, lest he lose his mind—and then, just as quickly as it had begun: silence. There was a small crackling of brush behind him, and he spun to meet a black figure rising from the night. He groped for the Colt.

"Be at ease, Samuel Peters," Lement spoke, his voice light and airy. "If I wished to kill you, you would be dead already."

"What do you want?"

"Just to talk. It's so seldom that I have the opportunity to converse with anyone. They usually just scream."

"What could we possibly have to talk about?"

"The dark," Lement said, his eyes gleaming even from out the shadows. "You know Sam, when you live in the dark long enough, it starts to speak to you. It shows you things. Strange and wondrous things. The world behind the world. But you already know that, don't you?"

"Yes."

"And what of your darkness, Sam? Does it show you things? What does it say?"

"It says *Lorraine*. That's all it ever says."

"Ah yes, Lorraine. Terrible thing, losing a loved one. But you know Sam, just because someone's gone doesn't mean we have to accept it. We need not submit to death. There are other paths one might pursue."

Sam looked up. "What do you mean?"

"What if she could be brought back?"

"No one can do that."

"I can," Lement corrected.

"No."

"Yes. And she would come back whole, Sam. Not a mere shade, not the spiritless, shriveled husk of a thing that has moldered beneath snows and summers and rains these last three years. No Sam, she would come back yours, as she was… If you would only help us, Sam, we know how to return a favor."

Sam remained silent.

"Well, take some time. Mull it over. But know I don't like to be kept waiting, Samuel Peters."

Lement was gone before the sound of his words had faded,

leaving Sam alone in the dark.

His sleep was troubled, hissing voices scraping through his head, shadowed forms skating across his mind's eye; white on black in jagged, kaleidoscopic patterns, then over red in deeps, falling.

He awoke shivering, having sweat through his sheets. Charlie whined from the end of the bed, got up and gave him a few licks on the cheek.

"I'm ok, buddy. It's all right," Sam said, petting him.

It was still dark, but he knew he wouldn't be able to get back to sleep. He got up and walked to the kitchen to put on coffee. Looking out the window to the east, Sam could see the first dull intimations of dawn gathering. He paced the living room, unable to shake the thought.

Could Lement's offer be real?

Why not?

It was only days ago that he hadn't believed in monsters.

Was resurrection such a leap when you considered that?

But at what cost?
He weighed it as he watched the day star rise.

It was mid morning by the time they finished loading up Sam's truck. Lenchner had gathered quite an arsenal; firebombs, dynamite, the old M1, a .375 Holland & Holland rifle with telescopic sight, an AR-15 with a hundred round drum magazine, a universe of assorted silver ammunition, flash grenades, a bag of stakes and mallets, two machetes and several flashlights.

"How long have you been doing this?" Sam asked as the truck rolled along toward the school.

"Since I was a young man," Lenchner said, holding the bag of stakes across his lap. "Since the end of the Second World War."

"And how did you get into it?"

Lenchner sighed. "I sought out others who had been left in their wake. They took me in, taught me all they knew, just as I have taught others over the years."

"Because of your family."

"At first," Lenchner said, staring out the window at the passing trees. "At first it was for my family. But then it was for all the families that had been, and all the families that were to come."

They parked several streets away from the old building, then hiked around the pond to its back. After watching the still grounds for about an hour they moved in, finding an unboarded window and climbing through.

"We start with the lower levels," Lenchner said clicking on a flashlight, "if they hear us milling around upstairs they'll have us cornered. We work our way up." He set a thin trip wire across the bottom of the window and rigged a flash grenade to it. "No surprise guests this way."

They worked their way past the main office and down the stairwell to the sublevel.

"The basement," Lenchner said, Sam leading on.

The boiler room was silent, save for the sound of their footsteps as they entered. Bloody footprints marked the floor leading to and from a storeroom next to the old boiler itself.

Sam readied his Colt and flashlight while Lenchner raised the machete, and moved for the door handle. It clicked, unlocked, and Sam shined the flashlight beam as Lenchner pulled the door open.

Within, on a pile of grubby gym mats, lay the pale forms of Grace Dreger and Tommy Richards, holding hands as they slept.

"My God," Sam whispered, "they're alive."

"Wait," Lenchner said, holding Sam back.

He shined his own flashlight on Grace's shoulder,

revealing a deep, ragged wound. He moved the beam to her face, her mouth messed with dark blood. Tommy was the same.

"I'm sorry, Sam," Lenchner said, tucking the machete back into its sheath. "There is no helping them."

"We can't just—"

"It is a mercy, I assure you."

He stared at the children.

"You don't have to do it, Sam. I will. But you'll need to hold the light for me."

Sam nodded, looking on as the old man set about his work. Grace was first.

He placed the stake over her heart unceremoniously and with one swift blow of the mallet drove it through. Her eyes opened with a flash of white as her body shriveled up, blood geysering out of her mouth.

Tommy stirred in his sleep, but did not wake.

Not until Lenchner repeated the act with him.

Then he severed the heads.

It took them the better part of the day to search the rest of the building, coming up with nothing. The sun was low in the west when they emerged from the school.

"The Master will not allow himself to be discovered so easily. I doubt even his familiars know where he's holed up," Lenchner said.

"Can we lure him out somehow?"

"Too risky. In the open he would be unstoppable."

"Then our only chance is to catch him at rest."

"Yes."

"Ok," Sam said. "Then tomorrow we start with all the condemned and abandoned buildings in town. There aren't many."

Lenchner nodded.

They made their way through the woods and back to the truck.

Terror came to Graves Harbor on silken wings.

Monique Andrews stirred in her sleep. She dreamt of walking a long, twisting hall—a hall of laughing, wheeling shadows—toward some indeterminable end. But then something—what was it? A door? Yes, a great door rose before her out of the dark. Its wood was carved with scenes of ancient lands and battles long forgotten, of horrors innumerable. Some of the figures moved, writhing in agony as she ran her hands over its surface. She found its great, twisted iron handle, and with all her strength turned it, a great bell resounding as the door unlocked.

It was blown open, throwing her back with an icy gust, opening onto a black, snow swept plain.

A figure stood before her, all but featureless in the dark.

But she could see it had knives for fingers, and glinting razors for teeth as its head rolled back, motioning for her to join it in the night.

She reached out, and with frozen daggers it accepted her pale hand, guiding her into its icy embrace.

Jackson Coombs awoke with a start, standing barefoot in the dirt shoulder down the road from his trailer.

Had he been sleepwalking?

The night was silent, save for the rustling swish of blowing grasses.

He had the sick, uncanny sense of being watched, and looking up into the trees above, he saw that their swaying branches were full of hundreds of silent, unmoving birds, staring on with black, unblinking eyes.

"What the—"

They took to the air in fluttering chaos, circling about him like a tempest, faster and faster, their fury mounting.

He knew—not understanding how—he simply knew, without a doubt, that they'd come to eat him alive; to tear him to carrion pieces.

He closed his eyes as they began to collect, merging into a black form, creeping up behind him, long, snow white fingers wrapping about his neck.

He turned, his scream staining the night.

"Sarge," Pete Morgan spoke through the screen door, looking out into the nighted yard. "What are you doing here, Sarge? You died in Korea. I saw you die."

"That's bullshit, Morgan," the green fatigued figure spoke, removing its helmet, rifle shining in the moonlight. "And what sort of way is that to address a superior?"

Pete snapped to attention, shooting up straight.

"Sorry, Sergeant."

"Now fall in for inspection, soldier. On the double."

"Yes, Sergeant," Pete said, opening the door and stepping out into the night, the dark swallowing him.

O'Connor was walking out of the station when he noticed the figure leaning against his Buick.

"Hey, buddy, get off my car."

"Oh, I'm sorry," Jacobi spoke, "I did not realize it was yours, Detective O'Connor."

"How do you know my name? Have we met?"

"No, but I believe you know my work."

O'Connor flicked the clasp off his holster.

"What do you mean by that?"

"Why, Cal Norris of course! I left him with quite a mug, didn't I? And that tasty strumpet Sophia Reardon, how did you like her?"

O'Connor pulled his pistol, but before he could level it Jacobi was off and running, across Thatchery Road and into the woods beyond. O'Connor gave chase.

He sprinted, brush and branches lashing his face as he hurdled through the forest, the night wind messing his dark hair.

How someone could move that fast, he did not know. The figure even stopped to look back several times, as if urging him on.

O'Connor emptied his gun at him, the shots echoing in the night.

But now his breath was labored, his lungs burning. His heart pounded and his sides ached. He tripped over a root and tumbled down into a gully, where he lay gasping beneath black, skeletal trees.

Then the coughing started, the wet, hacking convulsions. He covered his mouth with his hand, and when he pulled it away he saw it was speckled with dark blood. The world was spinning, and he let himself fall backward into the dry crackle of dead leaves.

"You know," Jacobi spoke, stepping down the drop and standing over him, "when I first started killing, I didn't feel much of anything about it. It was slightly arousing I suppose; to see something slow and cease. That was physical. But emotionally, I was void. It was only over the centuries that I began to savor it." Jacobi kneeled, wiping the wet hair off O'Connor's sweating forehead. "By modern psychological standards I was, and am, what is known as a sociopath. But to be honest, I find the term a bit reductive. I can empathize with the hunted, the haunted driven, with those who have run short on time." He opened his shirt, showing the man where his bullets had struck home. The dark wounds were healing, closing before him.

Wide eyed, O'Connor struggled to catch his breath, wiping the blood-strung spit from his mouth.

"I can help you with that," Jacobi spoke. "It's a relatively simple matter of you asking me to. You could live forever. And don't tell me you don't want that. I see you, O'Connor. I know your hunger intimately. It's in your face. You'd scream it if you could."

O'Connor nodded his head, and under great pain managed to whisper: "Yes."

Sam stared out the kitchen window, unable to sleep. The world had changed so much in so little time; he was having trouble keeping up with it.

Maybe the past few days had been one long dream.

Maybe he would wake up, put a bullet in the Colt, stick the barrel in his mouth and paint the walls with his brains.

Maybe he would wake up in jail for having aided in the killing of two children. Or a nuthouse, sweating out drugs and screaming at shadows.

He put his trembling hands on the window frame and leaned his face against the cool glass, closing his eyes.

"Please God," he prayed, "help me."

Minutes passed, and when he opened his eyes the first thing he saw was *her*. Lorraine. Lorraine in her garden, cloaked in darkness. Her hair had grown back, light brown, lush and curled, no longer sparse and gray from the chemo. She waved to him, beckoning as he stood paralyzed, as she turned gracefully and disappeared from sight.

Sam was startled from his trance by a loud bark, and turned just in time to see Charlie round the kitchen at breakneck speed. The dog leapt, breaking through the sliding glass door and tearing off into the night, howling after the apparition.

"Charlie!" Sam called, chasing the dog to the end of the yard where it turned into dense woods.

But Charlie was already gone.

And his resurrected wife nowhere to be seen.

He drove to the only place that made sense. The place he'd gone nearly every day for the last three years.

The Graves Harbor Cemetery; row thirty-eight, plot twelve.

And surely enough, the ground was opened, the earth heaped around the grave in great mounds. He looked over the edge to see the opened casket: empty.

He fell to his knees.

Lement had been true to his word.

Then, sliding out of the misted dark before him, there stepped Lorraine like something from a dream.

"Sam," her voice sounded, distant chimes in a soft wind. "I'm here, Sam."

Tears brimmed in his eyes, and words failed him.

"Do as they ask, Sam. It's the only way we can be together," she spoke, her white silk gown lifting on the night breeze. He longed, in that moment, more than anything, to be lost within those silken folds; lost with her in the dark. "Do as they ask and I'm yours."

"I will," he swore, finding his voice. "I'll do anything. Anything!"

Her eyes gleamed, and in an instant she was gone, vanished.

He rose with newfound resolve.

Anything.

The dawn found Graves Harbor much changed. Houses remained shut, blinds drawn, businesses—some of their windows boarded—did not open.

Jackson Coombs slept under a tarp on the cool floor of his garage, his fevered dreams full of blood and thirst undying.

In the belly of the dry docked sloop beside his house, Pete Morgan marveled at the renewed strength in his limbs, his arthritis seeming to have dissipated almost overnight. He felt as though fifty years had been lopped off his weary eighty— for the Master was kind.

The dank storeroom of Brockton's bar sheltered Patty Novak, Roger Kemp, and old Brockton himself, where they slept the sleep of a living death.

On the floor of his bedroom Earl continued his regeneration, though his new mind, having surfaced from the black, primeval depths of the unconscious, now knew nothing of life but hunger, pain, and savagery.

In their home on Juniper Drive, Monique Andrews sipped at a tall glass of her husband's still-warm blood, savoring it as a newborn would its mother's milk.

Graves Harbor lay quiet in the dawn.

O'Connor entered the police station to find Jim Parker behind the front desk, looking tired and drawn. He looked up.

"Good morning, Detective."

O'Connor stared at the man's neck, at the large vein that throbbed and quivered beneath the stubbled skin, begging to be opened.

"Detective?"

O'Connor pulled his pistol and shot Parker in the face, blood and brain matter spraying the white tile wall behind.

"Good morning, Deputy."

Hearing the shot, Hardiman came running down the hall, sidearm drawn.

O'Connor stepped around the corner to meet him.

"Hi, Sheriff. Deputy Jim's just taking a nap."

"What are you—"

He hooked three fingers into Hardiman's mouth and tore his jaw clean off, the man falling to the floor, seizing with shock.

O'Connor watched as he drowned in his own blood.

Sam called on Lenchner around midday, the old man opening the door to him. "Sam, come in," he said, turning back into the house. "I have been think—"

Sam hit him at the base of the skull with the butt of his Colt, Lenchner falling forward onto the hall carpet with a crash. He groaned as Sam pulled him into the library and bound him to a chair with strong rope.

"What... What are you..."

"Where is it?"

"What do you..."

"Where's the fucking amulet, Friedrich?"

"Oh, I see," the old man whispered, recovering his faculties. "Tell me Sam, how did they get to you?"

"I don't want to hurt you, Friedrich, but I don't think they will share my sympathy. Where is it?"

Lenchner laughed. "Somewhere. Somewhere in this funhouse. I wish you luck, I really do."

Sam sat down in a chair opposite, and together they waited for nightfall.

With the twilight they came forth, down darkened lanes and shadowed streets, pavement still warm from the day's sun. They came drunk on the fresh world that lay before them, a world that had always been there, just beyond reach—but no more. The night was a house of dark wonders.

They converged at the bottom of Lenchner's hill and surged up the deeply rutted road, dancing through the trees, howling and leaping. Earl sidled along on all fours toward the back of the party like an ape, growling and spitting, slamming his fists against his head, raving unintelligibly.

Soon, it was whispered among them, they would drink of the Master, and so seal their covenant; one with the Master, the new church, one with the dark. And soon, soon they would conquer the light, and all the world would tremble before them, before their radiance.

Sam and Lenchner stood in the doorway as the pale faces began to spill forth from the drive, forming into a circle around the house. Gleaming sets of eyes shone from the surrounding woods, the lower, meaner forms of life keeping a deliberate distance.

"You're making a mistake. Whatever they've offered you," Lenchner spoke. "They cannot be trusted."

"Just keep your mouth shut," Sam ordered, forcing the old man down the steps and into the dooryard.

"Where is Lement?" Sam shouted to the gathering rabble.

"Here," the vampire's voice sounded, Lement stepping forward as the crowd parted for him, Jacobi and O'Connor flanking his sides.

"The old man is yours. Now where is my wife?"

"I am a man of my word, Samuel Peters," Lement said, stepping aside as Lorraine, still clothed in white silk, came into view.

"Lorraine," Sam spoke, reaching out to her.

But as he did so her face began to twitch and shift, her short, light brown hair growing dark and long, skin shedding like a snake's to reveal Mara's wet, glistening visage beneath.

"No," Sam cried. "No, damn you, no!" He fell to his knees. "But her grave, where is her—"

"Her body?" Lement interjected. "At the town dump, of course. She belongs to the rats now, Samuel. They're gnawing at her as we speak."

Sam couldn't tell where the laughing began, whether it had been someone in the crowd, Jacobi or Mara, but it hadn't been Lement. No, the old monster just stared at him, smiling as the inhuman cackling rose higher and higher into the night, echoing down the hillside and through the surrounding woods.

He had been utterly deceived.

Sam pulled the Colt and emptied it into Lement, the silver slugs opening smoking holes in the vampire's chest. He was pushed back a few steps by the blows and stood, staring in bemusement.

"That hurt, Samuel," he spoke, digging one of the bullets out with two long nailed fingers. "Silver, eh?"

"Are you all right, father?" Jacobi asked, steadying him.

"Fine," Lement hissed, brushing Jacobi's hand away. "But I've lost my sense of humor with this one. O'Connor," he summoned, the man approaching. "Take this maggot heap into the wilderness and end him. Take your time with it."

"Yes, Master," O'Connor said. With unnatural quickness, he moved to where Sam knelt. Sam looked up through tear-blurred eyes to see a fist connect, the world cutting to black.

"Well," Lement spoke, stepping up to Lenchner, picking the remaining bullets out of his chest. "That just leaves you, old slayer."

"Guess so."

"I don't suppose you'd be willing to do this the easy way?"

Lenchner smiled. "A little late to start now, don't you think?"

Lement smiled in return. "I can respect that."

He turned to Jacobi. "Burn it down. We'll sift through the ashes."

"As you command, father."

Jacobi whistled, summoning Earl forth, the beast charging out of the crowd and bowing at his feet. A jug of gasoline was handed up.

"That's a good Earl," Jacobi praised, patting his head. He then poured the gas over him, Earl smiling and grunting as he did so. Jacobi struck a match and set him alight, the flames licking over with a whoosh.

"Go," he commanded.

The wailing torch of a man exploded forth in ecstatic agony, tearing up into the house and through its halls, crashing into furniture and walls and up the stairs into the second and third floors, setting off scores of traps, flying blades and razor wires. As he reached the third floor, Earl was little more than sheer momentum, his body bruised, diced, flayed and burnt beyond all recognition.

"I knew he'd be useful for something," Jacobi laughed.

The house began to roar up in flames, the familiars dancing around the structure in awful gesticulating leaps and poses, hips thrusting, arms slicing through the air like blades, inhuman cries leaping from their throats. Black figures against a towering blaze, traversing the night.

Sam was falling, the world tumbling past, and he had the uncanny notion that he might never find its solidity again. Then he did, with a hollow thump as his body connected with the dry forest floor. He brushed the filth out of his eyes and tried to reorient himself to his surroundings. He could tell by the forked path he lay in that he was at the bottom of Reacher's Hill, to the east of Lenchner's place.

He looked up to see O'Connor taking long, effortless strides down the face of the hill with sprightly, unnatural ease. Sam rolled to his side as the man reached the bottom, landing with a stomp where he'd lain.

"The Master said to make it slow," O'Connor said, grabbing him by the throat as easily as an adult would a small child. He lifted the struggling man into the air. "Just let me do the work."

He began to wail on Sam with his free hand, hard as a brick into his face, his sides, his chest, over and over—

explosions of pain. Sam was beginning to lose consciousness when he heard a low growl from the shadows. He opened his eyes just in time to see Charlie leap out of the night, sinking white fangs into O'Connor's arm.

"Ahhhhhh!"

O'Connor dropped Sam to a heap on the forest floor as Charlie continued to tear into his arm, refusing to let go.

Sam struggled to loose the hidden thirty-two from his leg holster while O'Connor and the dog struggled. He finally pulled it free, and leveled it in time to see O'Connor lifting Charlie over his head.

"Don't!" Sam shouted.

O'Connor smiled and brought the struggling dog down over his knee with an awful crunch, Charlie letting out a muted wail.

"No!" Sam cried, firing the handgun into O'Connor's head and chest, dropping him to the dirt. Sam leapt upon him and began to smash his face with the butt of the pistol, over and over again, until his hand was raw from it. O'Connor lay motionless, his skull reduced to bloody pulp. Sam pulled a knife from his boot and without thinking began to saw off what little remained of the man's head, until he heard a small whine from the dark to his left.

He turned, dropping the knife, and crawled to where Charlie lay.

Sam took the dog in his arms and cradled him, pressing their faces together.

"Charlie, it's ok, Charlie. It's going to be ok, it's…"

But it was obvious how badly broken the dog was, and

Sam could feel his breath slowing.

Charlie turned his brown eyes to Sam one last time, and Sam stroked his head.

"Shhh, Charlie boy," Sam said, eyes welling. "We can be quiet now. It's all right."

Charlie nuzzled in close.

"I love you, baby boy."

Then all Sam felt was weight.

And there followed rage.

When the house was little more than a smoldering hole in the ground, Lement ordered the familiars into the blistering ruin. The fevered smell of burning flesh filled the night air as they sifted, screaming, through the glowing embers in search of their prize.

Lement turned to face Lenchner.

"Just a matter of time, old slayer. And with the dawn comes our dominion."

"Abomination," Lenchner whispered in return.

"I don't know why you hate us so, old slayer. After all, it is your race that is the cancer of this world. War, pollution, overpopulation. *We* are the earth's true inheritors, Lenchner. We are balance."

Lenchner spat at Lement's feet, the vampire smiling.

"I do believe I'll crucify you, old slayer. Yes, and leave you for the birds. They will eat out your eyes and rend the flesh from your bones. I will smile upon the sight beneath the day star, and you will know the full measure of your failure."

A cry of relief sounded from the pit, and up was passed, in a line of raw, charred familiars, a small, blackened object. Jacobi approached with the treasure and kneeled before Lement.

"It is yours, father."

As dawn approached they made their way into the downtown, gathering at the intersection of Main and Thatchery. A soft rain had slicked the streets during the night, and steam rose up in swirling, ghostly vapors.

It was a perfect place for the ritual. There was a clear line of sight over the harbor to the east, so that the first rays of sun would reach them unobstructed.

The familiars, in various stages of regeneration from their baptism of fire, fashioned headpieces of wildflowers and swayed on blistered feet in dreamy anticipation.

They would be the first to receive the new blood.

Acolytes of the Master—of the new church.

A group of them gleefully took up the task of crucifying Lenchner, using the large cross that stood on the lawn of First Methodist.

The old man remained stoic for it, though he bit through his lip as they drove the wide nails into his wrists and feet, the hot blood running in sticky streams.

Mara and Jacobi undressed Lement with reverence, and the vampire stepped forward from the crowd, looking out across the water to the east. The day had come. Their reclamation. The assumption of their rightful place in the great order. The rise of an empire— one of blood and horror. He would be hailed as a benefactor of their species, his authority amongst the clans assured.

He raised the amulet to the sky, Jacobi and Mara undressing and flanking his sides as he did so.

The familiars bowed in silence.

And as the dull swelling of the light peaked over the horizon, an ethereal luminescence—a shade beyond the known spectrum—began to emanate from the amulet's stone, washing over them in undulating waves, like water, accompanied by an audible, vibratory throb. The quickening air seemed to thicken with soft, humming electricity, the smell of blood and iron filling their nostrils.

"Yes," Lement whispered, basking in the heat. "Yes."

Their physical forms began to alter, as if in their concentration some sort of aesthetic guard had been dropped, their true nature revealing itself. Their faces grew pointed, noses flattening to slits. Their jaws sagged, teeth lengthening. Wet, glistening membranes formed between long fingers. They became hunched, the nubs of their vertebrae growing sharp, rising through the skin in great curling spines. Their skin took on a hideous translucence.

Just below the otherworldly pulse, the low drone of a car motor rose. Jackson Coombs turned to see a truck approaching down Thatchery, others turning with him.

Sam lit the short fuse and opened the door, tossing the .375 and a supply bag out. Gripping the AR-15, he jumped, rolling to the road's grassy shoulder.

The truck continued its downhill trajectory, the familiars beginning to scatter.

He'd timed it perfectly, the fuse burning down almost exactly as the truck reached the intersection.

Loaded with most of Lenchner's dynamite, as well as several hundred pounds of tools from Johnson's hardware shop, the truck was essentially a five-thousand pound rolling claymore.

The roar was tremendous, the explosion shaking the street, shattering every window along Main.

A flying bumper tore Roger Kemp in half.

A ball bearing caught Monique Andrews in the back of the head, her face opening like a flower.

The intersection took on the semblance of a nightmare. Maimed, twisted forms wandered through smoke and fire. Bodies lay strewn, severed and smashed, burned beyond recognition.

Patty Novak groped wildly at his face, most of it missing. One eye gaped, wide and panicked, as his cries gurgled out.

"Glurrrrrrrr! Mahhhhhhhhhhgluuuuuuurrrrrr!"

Engulfed in flames, a screaming Jackson Coombs writhed on the pavement, trying in vain to extinguish himself.

Slinging the AR-15 over his shoulder, Sam aimed the .375 through the smoke, lining the sights up with Lement.

Come on. Come on.

The shot rang out, echoing over the harbor, the vampire's head blowing open with a spray of dark blood. Lement collapsed in the street, the amulet flying from his grasp and dropping down a storm grate, whatever otherworldly power it summoned dissipating with a thunderclap.

The sun was well over the horizon now, and Lenchner was laughing.

"How do you like it, old monster?! Is it all you dreamed?!"

Lement was hissing, clawing frantically as his progeny struggled to drag him out of the light.

"Father!" Jacobi cried, his skin blistering, peeling away in sheets.

Lement gasped, a ragged, serpentine rattle. His black eyes—gone over white—sank back in his skull, smoke pouring from the sockets. With a heaving convulsion, his body came apart in a pile of black, smoldering embers.

"Nooooooo!" Mara howled, falling to her knees.

"Come!" Jacobi shouted, pulling her along with him across the sun-drenched street and breaking through the storefront of Carpenter's Nautical shop.

Sam dropped the .375, taking up the AR-15 and running toward the church, firing at the last of the fleeing familiars.

"Come back have you?" Lenchner laughed.

"I'm sorry," Sam said, supporting his weight, wrenching the nails loose. "They tricked—"

"I know what they did. It doesn't matter now."

Sam helped him down and to a nearby bench.

"Where are the other two?" Sam asked as he tore the sleeve of his shirt off to make bandages.

"Carpenter's," Lenchner said, wincing with pain.

After dressing the old man's wounds, Sam turned as if to go in.

"No," Lenchner said, grabbing him by the arm. "You're no match for them. Even wounded."

"So what do we do?"

The old man grinned.

Sam lit the remaining dynamite and heaved it through the smashed storefront window. He then ran back to where Lenchner sat and moved him farther away.

It took thirty seconds for the fuse to burn down, wood, brick and glass flying with a resounding boom.

When all had settled Sam walked over to inspect the smoking ruin.

A pile of brick turned over, a ragged form crawling out from beneath, black and twisted.

Jacobi hissed, and was about to say something as Sam opened fire, riddling him with bullets, spent shells tinkling on the pavement. When the gun clicked empty he dropped it, pulling a stake out of his boot. What little was left of the vampire was still trying to slither away when Sam drove the sharpened wood through, piercing his ancient heart. Jacobi crumbled to filth.

Sam walked around back of the building, where he found Mara trying to crawl beneath a station wagon.

He pulled her out by what remained of her legs.

"Wait," she cried, but he had already begun to stab her. Not once, but again and again, viciously—a staggering, primal cry rising in his throat—until he struck home, her body shriveling up beneath him like burning leaves.

Sam looked up, staring in silence across the harbor into the rising sun. Ashes swirled about him on the morning breeze.

After some minutes he got up and walked over to the storm grate, finding the amulet caught between the bars. He returned to Lenchner, handing over the relic.

"What about the others?"

"Without the Master's blood the infection will kill them. A few days and it will be over."

Lenchner looked over at Lement's remains.

"They're us, you know. Through a dark glass."

The two men stared on in silence. Smoke curled into the cloudless blue sky overhead.

"What about the amulet?" Sam asked after some minutes had passed.

"I leave it in your charge," Lenchner said, handing it back with a weary smile. "I've gotten too old for this dance."

Sam helped the old man to his feet, supporting him as they walked in silence up Thatchery, their shadows stretching long and dark before them.

About the Author:

W.J. Renehan is the Editorial Director of Dark Hall Press, a publisher of first-rate Horror and Science Fiction. His book *The Art of Darkness: Meditations on the Effect of Horror Fiction* is available from New Street Communications, LLC. He is an alumnus of Dean College, SUNY New Paltz, and the University of Rhode Island.

DARK HALL PRESS

Dark Hall seeks to promote a diverse body of quality works, advancing the tradition of Horror storytelling as well as providing exposure for up-and-coming writers.

Visit us online at

darkhallpress.com